ECHO
Surviving the Silence

EX KATSAROS

Table of Contents

Dedication

To the whisperers, the forgotten songs, and the echoes of civilizations lost to the currents of time. This is for those whose stories, though silenced, still reverberate through the cosmic tapestry, a testament to the enduring power of memory and the interconnectedness of all things. For those who dared to dream of a universe where the hum of existence isn't drowned out by the deafening roar of oblivion, but rather, resonates with a symphony of shared experience and consciousness, however faint or fragmented. This is dedicated to the unwavering belief in the enduring strength of hope, even in the face of cosmic indifference.

It is for the lost voices, the untold narratives, and the enduring mysteries of the universe that continue to inspire us to search for truth, even when the very fabric of reality is threatened. It is for the dreamers, the seekers, the explorers, who, with unwavering resolve, continue to traverse the labyrinthine passages of existence, relentlessly following the whispers of the past, and searching for the echoes of a greater truth in the vast emptiness of the cosmos. For the brave souls who search for meaning in the silent spaces between stars, for those who recognize the beauty in the fragility of life, and for those who find solace in the quiet

hum of the cosmos - this story is for you. This book is a testament to the human capacity for resilience, the unyielding pursuit of truth, and our profound connection to something far greater than ourselves. May this narrative serve as a reminder that even in the face of unimaginable loss, the echoes of what once was can still guide us towards a future worth fighting for. For the quiet courage found in the face of overwhelming odds, for the tenacity that stems from a belief in a better tomorrow, and for the unyielding spirit of humanity that transcends even the seemingly insurmountable, this story is humbly dedicated.

The Transport

The old engines of the Starseeker made a loud and unending rusty noise, a constant companion, matching the nervous moments of the young guards Jax and Rix watching over Echo's transport. They were young, just finished their training, their faces betraying a mixture of apprehension and showing clear signs of fear. Echo, in contrast, sat serenely in her containment cell, a picture of unsettling calm amidst the metallic clang and hum of the ship's failing systems. Her deep blue eyes were deep and full of mystery making her look indifferent from the nervous energy around her. Shain, leaning against the wall, observed them all with a weary cynicism that had become second nature.

The Starseeker wasn't a luxury liner; it was a repurposed freighter, its hull scarred by countless interstellar journeys and patched with jury-rigged repairs. Shain, with his grizzled face and the slouched weariness in his posture, was the perfect reflection of the ship itself—worn, but still functional, still capable of cutting through the dangers of deep space. He ran a calloused hand over his stubbled chin, the rhythmic scraping a small comfort in the tense atmosphere. The flickering lights, casting long, dancing shadows across the cramped corridor, added to the unsettling ambiance. He'd seen enough containment breaches in

his career to know that even the most secure cell could fail, and the thought sent a shiver down his spine.

He wasn't worried about Echo escaping; not in the traditional sense. Her eerie passivity was more unsettling than any violent outburst could ever be. What concerned him was the official narrative surrounding her capture, the thin veil of plausible deniability woven by the Galactic Council. The report, a dry, impersonal document, spoke of a "metaphysical weapon" and a "psychic plague," terms that felt more like euphemisms than factual descriptions. Shain, a man of practicality, preferred concrete facts to vague pronouncements. Years ago, a similar incident had shaken his faith in the Council's transparency, and he'd been harboring a deep-seated suspicion ever since. That incident involved a political prisoner, framed for treason, who'd been transported under similar circumstances. The prisoner had vanished without a trace, and the Council's official report had conveniently glossed over the matter.

He glanced at Echo once more, her stillness a sharp contrast to the restless energy of the two young guards. Jax nervously checked his pulse rifle, the faint click echoing in the confined space. Rix fidgeted with the containment cell's locking mechanism, his unease written all over his jerky movements. Shain understood their nervousness; the Iridian annihilation on Luna Minor was a cataclysmic event, a wiping out of an entire colony—200,000 souls erased from existence. The whispers of it were a constant background hum in the galaxy's political arena, a story that resonated with fear and uncertainty.

But there was something profoundly wrong about Echo's demeanor. There was an eerie stillness to her, an absence of despair that should be expected from the sole survivor of such a devastating event. It was this absence, this unsettling calm, that fueled Shain's growing unease. It wasn't the quiet of grief or shock; it was a deeper, more ancient silence, a silence that seemed to hum with subtle energy, a low thrum that was almost imperceptible but felt deep in his bones.

He knew the risks involved in defying the Council. He was a marshal, part of the vast machinery of the galaxy, and questioning its directives was a dangerous game. But the inconsistencies in the official narrative, coupled with Echo's unsettling composure, had planted a seed of doubt in his mind— one that was rapidly growing into a suspicion he couldn't shake. He needed answers to his concerns. He needed to know everything about the incident on Luna Minor. The Council's narrative seemed too convenient, too neatly packaged, to be believable.

His past experiences had made him unsympathetic, made him wary of authority, and cynical of justice. He'd seen the machinations of power, the corruption that festered within the very systems he was sworn to uphold. He remembered a young idealistic recruit, brimming with zeal for making right what was wrong, a naïve faith in the system that the grim realities of galactic politics had systematically eroded. That recruit, that young man full of hope, had been worn down by the grind, the endless cycle of injustice and compromise, leaving only a weary cynicism in his wake. He was that worn-down man now,

skeptical of everything but still driven by a reluctant sense of duty.

The ship bucked slightly, a jarring jolt that sent a tremor through the corridor. Jax and Rix reacted instantly, hands tightening on their weapons. Echo didn't even flinch. She simply sat there, her eyes closed, as if oblivious to the jarring motion of the Starseeker, a testament to the unsettling calm that had consumed her ever since her capture.

Shain rubbed his temples, the dull ache settled as a familiar companion, reflecting the constant pressure and weight of his ever-growing doubts. He found himself staring at the faded star charts plastered on the bulkhead. They were ancient, their colors muted with age. Each faint line and constellation whispered of forgotten journeys, of civilizations long since vanished. It was a poignant reminder of the ephemerality of existence, a stark counterpoint to the enduring mysteries that surrounded Echo and the eradication of the Iridian colony.

The rhythmic hum of the Starseeker's engines continued, and the metallic groaning felt like a constant drone. The journey ahead would be long and perilous, with an unpaved path, untold dangers, and unanswered questions. The weight of it pressed down on him, the weight of a mission that seemed to unravel every thread of his understanding, every certainty he had ever held dear. He took a deep breath, steeling himself for what was to come, the silence broken only by the relentless hum of the ancient freighter and the faint, inexplicable thrum emanating from Echo's cell. The truth, he sensed, lay hidden somewhere within that unsettling silence, waiting to be unearthed. And he,

against the odds and the counsel of the galaxy's most powerful organization, was determined to find it no matter what.

Shain's thoughts were interrupted by a sharp crackle from the comms panel, a burst of static that cut through the corridor's drone. Rix flinched, nearly dropping his toolkit, while Jax's rifle snapped up, his eyes darting to the shadows. "What was that?" Jax whispered, his voice tight with nerves.

Shain crossed to the panel, his fingers brushing the worn controls. The screen flickered, displaying a fragmented signal—short, encrypted bursts, pulsing like a heartbeat. "Rix, run a trace," Shain ordered, his voice steady but laced with urgency. "This isn't standard interference."

Rix's hands moved quickly, his youthful anxiety giving way to focus. "It's coming from the ship's auxiliary systems, sir. Not our comms grid—something external, piggybacking on our relays." His brow furrowed as he pulled up the data. "The encryption's not Council standard. It's... older, more complex. I've never seen anything like it."

Shain's gut twisted. He'd encountered similar signals once before, on a mission to Sylara, a lush planet of crystalline caves and whispering winds. He'd been sent to retrieve a rogue scientist, Vara Tyn, who'd claimed the Council was suppressing knowledge of a "cosmic resonance" that linked all life. Vara had been frantic, her eyes wild as she showed him a device emitting a similar signal—a low, harmonic pulse that seemed to vibrate in his chest. Shain had dismissed her, handing her over to the Council's enforcers. Days later, Sylara's research outpost was

destroyed, labeled a "technical malfunction." Vara's fate was a blank, another ghost in Shain's past, her warnings now echoing in the Starseeker's signal.

"Keep it isolated," Shain told Rix. "Don't let it spread to the main systems." He turned to Echo's cell, her eyes now open, fixed on him with an intensity that made his skin prickle. "You know what this is, don't you?" he asked, his voice low.

Echo's lips parted, her voice a soft hum that seemed to weave through the air. "It's a fragment, Shain. A piece of the song, calling out. They're listening, but they can't silence it completely." Her words were cryptic, yet they carried a weight that settled deep in his bones, stirring the same unease he'd felt on Sylara.

"What song?" Shain pressed, stepping closer to the containment field. "What are you carrying that's worth this?"

Echo's gaze softened, a flicker of sorrow breaking through her calm. "The universe's voice. The Iridians heard it, lived it. It's why they fear me—why they fear us all." She paused, her eyes searching his. "You've felt it too, haven't you? In the quiet, in the spaces between."

Shain's breath caught. He wanted to dismiss her words, to cling to the logic that had anchored him through years of service. But that hum, that faint vibration from her cell, was undeniable—a resonance that seemed to tug at memories he couldn't place. He shook his head, stepping back. "I need facts, Echo. Not riddles."

Her smile was faint, almost pitying. "The facts are in the silence, Shain. Listen closer."

Before he could respond, the ship lurched violently, a deep groan echoing through the hull. Alarms blared, red lights pulsing in the corridor. Jax stumbled, catching himself against the wall, while Rix scrambled to the nearest terminal. "Sir, it's the reactor core!" Rix shouted. "Power fluctuations—something's tampering with the stabilization grid."

Shain's heart raced. He sprinted to the terminal, pulling up the diagnostics. The reactor's output was spiking, a pattern too deliberate for a mechanical failure. "Sabotage," he muttered, his mind flashing to the encrypted signal. "Rix, lock it down. Jax, secure the corridor. Nobody moves until we know what's happening."

As Rix worked, Shain's eyes drifted to the crew roster on the terminal. A name caught his attention: Ensign Kaelis, a recent transfer, quiet and unassuming, assigned to engineering. Shain had noticed Kaelis lingering near the reactor bay during the last shift, his movements too precise, too deliberate. A memory flickered—on Sylara, a junior officer had betrayed Vara's team, planting a device that triggered the outpost's destruction. Was Kaelis a plant? An Eradicator agent?

"Rix, pull Kaelis's logs," Shain ordered, his voice tight. "Every access, every move."

Rix nodded, his fingers flying. "He's been in the reactor bay three times this cycle, sir. No logged reason. And... there's a biometric

anomaly in his profile. His neural signature's off, like it's being masked."

Shain's blood ran cold. He signaled Jax, who was already moving, rifle raised. "We're going to engineering. Now." They navigated the Starseeker's twisting corridors, the flickering lights casting eerie shadows. The hum from Echo's cell seemed to follow them, a faint pulse that kept Shain's nerves on edge.

In the reactor bay, the air was thick with ozone, the core's hum distorted by a low, dissonant whine. Kaelis stood at a control panel, his hands moving with unnatural speed. "Kaelis!" Shain barked, his rifle trained. "Step away."

Kaelis turned, his eyes unnaturally vacant, like polished glass. "You can't stop it," he said, his voice flat, mechanical. "The Silence demands her." A device in his hand pulsed, its runes matching the signal's encryption.

Jax lunged, tackling Kaelis before he could activate the device. Shain wrested it from his grip, its surface cold and slick, vibrating with a frequency that made his teeth ache. Rix scanned it, his face paling. "It's an Eradicator disruptor, sir. Designed to overload the reactor, take out the ship."

Shain's mind raced. The Eradicators weren't just watching—they were infiltrating, planting agents to ensure Echo never reached her destination. He disabled the device, its whine fading, but the reactor's fluctuations persisted. "Echo," he said through the comms, "this disruptor—it's tied to the signal. Can you counter it?"

Her voice came, calm but urgent. "The song can break it, Shain. Focus on the hum, the pulse you felt. Sing it with me."

Shain hesitated, his practical mind rebelling against the idea. But the hum was there, undeniable, resonating in his chest. He closed his eyes, letting it guide him, a vibration that seemed to align with the ship's rhythm. Jax and Rix watched, wide-eyed, as Shain hummed, the sound low and unsteady at first, then stronger, syncing with the reactor's pulse. The fluctuations stabilized, the alarms silencing one by one.

Kaelis, restrained by Jax, convulsed, his eyes clearing. "I didn't know," he gasped. "They... they were in my head." Shain's jaw tightened. An implant, controlling him like a puppet. He ordered Kaelis to the medbay, under guard, and returned to Echo's cell.

"You knew," Shain said, his voice a mix of awe and frustration. "You knew the song could do that."

Echo's eyes were gentle, but her words were firm. "It's not just power, Shain. It's truth. The Eradicators fear it because it binds us, makes us whole. They'll do anything to break that bond."

Shain's cynicism cracked, just a fraction. The song wasn't just a myth—it was a force, a defiance against the Council's lies. But the incident with Kaelis raised new questions. How many others were compromised? And what was the signal's source? He ordered a full sweep of the crew's biometrics, his trust in his own team shaken.

The Starseeker's journey took them past the Sylaran Nebula, a swirling expanse of violet and gold that seemed to pulse with its

own rhythm. Shain had avoided it since Vara's mission, its beauty tainted by guilt. But now, the nebula's glow seemed to echo the hum from Echo's cell, stirring a memory of Vara's device—a crystal that sang with the same frequency. Was it connected to the Iridian song? To Echo?

He approached the bridge, where Rix was analyzing the signal's origin. "It's not just external," Rix said, his voice low. "It's coming from the nebula, sir. A repeating pattern, like a beacon. And it's… responding to her." He nodded toward Echo's cell.

Shain's pulse quickened. He activated the ship's long-range sensors, focusing on the nebula. The data showed a faint anomaly—a sentient rift within the mists, its energy fluctuating in sync with Echo's hum. "A cosmic resonance," Vara had called it. Shain had scoffed then, but now he wasn't so sure.

He returned to Echo, the nebula's glow visible through the viewport. "That signal," he said, "it's tied to you, to the nebula. What's out there?"

Echo's gaze drifted to the swirling mists. "The Sylaran Nebula is a guardian, Shain. It holds fragments of the song, scattered when Luna Minor fell. The Eradicators can't touch it, but they're trying to corrupt it." Her voice dropped, almost a whisper. "There's a sanctuary beyond it—Valthara, where the Resonance Key waits."

Shain's breath caught. Valthara, a name from the Council's redacted files, a system marked as "uninhabited" after a supposed plague. The same files had mentioned a relic, dismissed as folklore. "The Resonance Key," he said. "What is it?"

"A crystal," Echo replied, "forged in the heart of Luna Minor. It amplifies the song, connects worlds. The Silent Choir protects it, but the Eradicators know it's there. They'll burn stars to stop us."

Shain's mind raced. The Silent Choir—an unknown group, allies or enemies? He ordered Rix to chart a course through the nebula, avoiding the rift's core. The Starseeker groaned, its systems strained by the nebula's energies. Jax, now more confident, took the helm, his hands steady despite the tension.

As they entered the nebula, the hum from Echo's cell grew stronger, vibrating through the hull. Shain felt it in his chest, a call he couldn't ignore. But the sensors blipped—a shadow in the mists, a ship, its signature matching Eradicator tech. "Brace for contact," Shain ordered, his voice cutting through the bridge's silence.

The enemy ship emerged, sleek and black, its hull etched with the same runes as Kaelis's device. It didn't fire, but a message crackled through the comms: "Surrender the Iridian, or the Silence takes you all." The voice was cold, mechanical, but human—a rogue Council operative, perhaps, or an Eradicator agent.

Shain's hand hovered over the weapons console, but Echo's voice stopped him. "Don't fight, Shain. Sing."

He stared at her, incredulous, but the hum was undeniable, growing stronger with the nebula's pulse. Jax joined in, his voice hesitant but resonant, a harmony that made the air shimmer. Shain added his own, clumsy at first, the vibration syncing with

the ship's systems. The enemy ship faltered, its sensors flickering, then retreated into the mists.

The Starseeker pressed on, the nebula's glow fading behind them. Shain slumped in his chair, exhausted but exhilarated. The song had saved them, but the threat remained. He looked at Echo, her calm unshaken. "Valthara," he said. "We're going there. But I need to know—who's the Silent Choir?"

"They're us," Echo said, her eyes gleaming. "Survivors, singers, scattered but unbroken. They guard the Key, waiting for the song to return."

Shain nodded, his cynicism battling a flicker of hope. The Starseeker's engines roared, carrying them toward Valthara, toward a truth that could unravel the galaxy—or save it. The hum from Echo's cell was a constant now, a reminder that the song was alive, and he was part of it, whether he believed or not.

Echo's Silence

The rhythmic hum emanating from Echo's cell reverberated through Shain, a deep subsonic vibration that seemed to seep into his very bones. It was more like a constant, unsettling reminder of the enigma she represented. He watched her, leaning against the bulkhead, his gaze fixed on her seemingly still form. But, even in her apparent stillness, there were subtle movements, barely perceptible shifts in posture, a twitch of a finger, and the almost imperceptible dilation of her pupils—hints of a hidden inner world struggling to break free. Her silence wasn't empty; it was heavy with an unspoken weight, a deep sadness that seemed to emanate from some ancient, forgotten wellspring. It was a sadness that transcended the mere loss of her people; it spoke of something far larger, far older. It was the sadness of a universe weeping for itself.

Her eyes, a deep, fathomless blue, held a depth that unnerved him. They reflected not just the cold light of the ship's interior but something far more significant—a cosmos of swirling galaxies, a universe of lost hopes and shattered dreams. They were the eyes of someone who had seen too much, who had witnessed the unraveling of reality itself. And in those eyes, Shain saw a reflection of his own weariness, a shared burden of

disillusionment. He had spent years navigating the murky depths of the galactic prison system, witnessing the machinations of power and the callous disregard for justice that had slowly eroded his idealism. He'd traded hope for cynicism, a process as inevitable as the sun's setting.

A sudden memory pierced through the haze, sharp and vivid—one from the early days of his career when he firmly believed in the system. He remembered a young prisoner, wrongly accused, his eyes burning with an incandescent rage that was later extinguished by the slow, grinding process of the prison's legal system. The prisoner, a brilliant astrophysicist, had been framed for treason, his groundbreaking research was deemed a threat to the Council's power. Shain had witnessed his spirit slowly crushed under the weight of fabricated evidence and relentless persecution. The memory stirred a raw sense of injustice within him, a burning resentment towards the corruption that he had become all too familiar with.

He'd seen countless other instances of manipulation and injustice during his career, where the powerful trampled on the weak, where truth was twisted and justice was denied. He'd learned to navigate this system with weary cynicism, to protect himself from the crushing weight of its injustices. But now, confronted by Echo, by the enigma surrounding the annihilation of the Iridians, his past experiences had become a new lens, focusing his understanding on a different level. He saw a pattern, a subtle echo of the manipulations he had witnessed so many times before—a rewriting of history, a silencing of truth.

There was a deep silence between him and Echo, a palpable tension that hung thick in the air, as if the very space between them held a weight of its own. It was a silence filled with unspoken questions, great accusations, fears left unsaid. It was the silence of shared trauma, of collective loss, echoing the emptiness of space itself. He could almost hear the whispers of the erased Iridians, their voices faint but persistent, carried on the cosmic winds—a tragic symphony accompanying the hum of the engines.

Another flashback caught over him: a dimly lit interrogation room, a gaunt figure slumped in a chair, his eyes hollow with despair. It was a witness, someone who had seen too much, someone who had dared speak the truth. A low-level bureaucrat, who knew of a corrupt deal between the Council and a shadowy organization. His testimony had been dismissed as inconsequential, his evidence deemed insignificant, his claims labeled as the ravings of a madman. Within months, he was dead—ruled an accident, his death quietly swept under the rug of galactic politics.

Shain closed his eyes, the memories a relentless assault on his weary soul. He'd seen the system's cruelty at close range and experienced its ruthless efficiency in silencing dissent and suppressing truth. He'd seen the masks of authority crumble to reveal the gaping maw of corruption. He'd learned that in the vast expanse of the galaxy, truth was often a fragile thing, easily crushed by the weight of power. And now, confronted by Echo by the horrifying mystery of the Iridians' annihilation, he found himself questioning the foundations of everything he thought he knew.

He opened his eyes, his gaze returning to Echo. She remained motionless, her breathing barely perceptible; her aura indicated a strange mixture of calm and profound sorrow. The silence intensified, a cosmic vacuum stretching the space between them. But, there was something else, something beneath the sadness, a glimmer of hope, a resilient spark that refused to be extinguished. It was the stubborn will of a survivor, a testament to the indomitable spirit of a people who refused to be erased. It reflected his internal struggle—the battle between cynicism and a reluctant sense of justice.

He was no longer just transporting a prisoner; he was escorting a symbol, a living testament to a truth the Council was desperate to bury. The burden of that truth pressed down on him, almost unbearable in its weight. He glanced out the viewport at the swirling nebulae, their vibrant colors a stark contrast to the dreary monotony of the Starseeker's interior. Those nebulae represented endless possibilities, unknown universes, yet here he was, bound to this grim mission. Yet, somehow, he felt a flicker of hope, a whisper of defiance. The journey was far from over, and the truth, he sensed, was just beginning to unfold. The silence, though heavy, would not last forever. Soon, it would be shattered by the storm that was brewing. The Eradicators were coming.

The hum from Echo's cell grew stronger, a pulse that seemed to sync with Shain's heartbeat, pulling him from his reverie. He straightened, his fingers brushing the cold metal of the bulkhead, grounding himself in the present. The Starseeker's journey through the Sylaran Nebula had heightened the crew's tension,

the aftermath of the Eradicator encounter still raw. Kaelis, the compromised ensign, was confined to the medbay, his implant removed but his mind fragile, a living reminder of the enemy's reach. Shain's trust in his crew was fraying, each face a potential mask for betrayal.

He approached Echo's cell, the containment field's faint shimmer a barrier between them. "That hum," he said, his voice low, rough with exhaustion. "It's not just you, is it? It's... alive, somehow."

Echo's eyes opened, their blue depths catching the nebula's glow through the viewport. "It's the song, Shain," she said, her voice a soft melody that seemed to weave through the air. "It's the universe's pulse, carried by my people, now scattered in fragments. You felt it in the nebula, didn't you? When you sang."

Shain's jaw tightened. The memory of humming with Echo and Jax, countering the Eradicator ship, was vivid—a moment of connection that defied his rational mind. "I don't understand it," he admitted. "But I felt it. Like it was pulling me somewhere."

Echo leaned forward, her fingers brushing the containment field, sparking a faint ripple. "It's pulling you to the truth. The song isn't just sound—it's memory, connection, life. The Eradicators silenced it on Luna Minor, but it lives in places like Valthara, in relics like the Echo Stone."

"The Echo Stone?" Shain's brow furrowed, his mind flashing to Vara Tyn's crystal on Sylara, its pulse so like the hum he felt now. "Is it like the Resonance Key?"

Echo nodded, her expression solemn. "The Key is the heart, amplifying the song across worlds. The Echo Stone is its shadow, a fragment that holds memories of the Iridians. It's hidden, protected by the Silent Choir, but the Eradicators hunt it too."

Shain's pulse quickened. Another relic, another piece of the puzzle. He recalled a mission on Thalara, a planet of glowing spires and harmonic winds, where he'd arrested a mystic, Lira Vex, who'd spoken of "singing stones" that guarded ancient truths. Lira's words had been dismissed, her enclave razed in a "structural collapse." Another ghost, another warning he'd ignored. "Where is it?" he asked. "This Echo Stone."

Echo's gaze drifted to the nebula. "In the Sylaran Rift, where the nebula's heart pulses. The Silent Choir guards it, but the Eradicators are close. They've corrupted the nebula's song, twisting its rhythm to hide their movements."

Before Shain could press further, a sharp alarm blared, the ship's lights flickering red. Jax burst into the corridor, his face pale. "Sir, it's the crew. Some are refusing orders, saying we're cursed, that she's the curse." He nodded toward Echo, his eyes conflicted. "They're talking mutiny."

Shain's stomach dropped. The nebula's pulse, the Eradicators' influence—it was unraveling his crew. He strode to the bridge, finding a dozen crewmembers gathered, their faces a mix of fear and defiance. Ensign Taryn, a wiry comms officer, stood at the forefront, her voice sharp. "We're flying into a trap, Captain. That signal, her humming—it's messing with our heads. We should turn back."

Shain's hand rested on his pulse pistol, his voice steady but cold. "You're scared, Taryn. I get it. But we're not turning back. Echo's not the enemy—the Eradicators are. You've seen what they did to Kaelis."

Taryn's eyes narrowed. "And what if she's controlling you? You're different since she came aboard. Obsessed."

Jax stepped forward, his voice firm. "She saved us in the nebula, Taryn. I felt it—the song. It's real, and it's not a curse." Shain glanced at Jax, surprised by his conviction, a spark of the song's influence in his eyes.

The tension broke as Rix's voice crackled through the comms. "Captain, we've got a problem in the nav core. Someone's tampering with the jump coordinates—rerouting us toward an Eradicator beacon."

Shain's blood ran cold. He ordered Jax to secure the bridge and led a team to the nav core, a cramped chamber pulsing with the ship's heartbeat. There, he found Ensign Vorn, a quiet technician, hunched over the controls, his hands moving with unnatural speed. "Vorn, step away," Shain barked, his pistol raised.

Vorn turned, his eyes glassy, like Kaelis's had been. "The Silence calls," he whispered, a device in his hand pulsing with Eradicator runes. Shain lunged, disarming him, but the device activated, sending a surge through the nav core. The Starseeker lurched, its systems flickering as the Sylaran Nebula's pulse intensified outside.

"Echo!" Shain called through the comms. "The song—can it stop this?"

Her voice came, calm but urgent. "Sing with me, Shain. Jax, too. Focus on the Stone's rhythm."

Shain closed his eyes, grasping for the hum, Jax joining him in a shaky harmony. The vibration grew, syncing with the nebula's pulse, countering the device's dissonance. The nav core stabilized, the coordinates realigning to Valthara. Vorn collapsed, his eyes clearing, his voice trembling. "They made me... I didn't know."

Shain restrained Vorn, his mind racing. The Eradicators were infiltrating minds, using the nebula's corrupted song. He returned to Echo, her calm unshaken. "The Echo Stone," he said. "We need it. Can it lead us to Valthara?"

Echo nodded. "It's a beacon, Shain. The Silent Choir will guide us, but the nebula's rift is dangerous. The Eradicators have a traitor among them—a Council operative, Veyra, who seeks the Stone for power."

Shain's jaw tightened. Veyra—a name from a redacted file, a rogue operative tied to Sylara's destruction. Another ghost, now a threat. He ordered Rix to scan the nebula for the Stone's signal, the sensors picking up a faint pulse, deep in the rift. The Starseeker's course was set, but the crew's unrest lingered, a fracture Shain couldn't ignore.

On the bridge, Jax approached, his expression torn. "Sir, I felt it again—the song. It's in me, like it's always been there. But it scares me. What if Taryn's right?"

Shain gripped Jax's shoulder, his voice firm. "It's not a curse, Jax. It's a gift. You're part of this, same as me. We trust Echo, we trust the song, and we get to Valthara."

Jax nodded, his resolve strengthening. Shain turned to the viewport, the nebula's mists swirling like a cosmic dance. The hum from Echo's cell was a constant now, a thread connecting him to Jax, to the crew, to the Silent Choir. But the Eradicators were closing in, their traitor Veyra a shadow in the rift. Shain's cynicism battled a growing hope, a belief that the song could defy the silence. The truth was out there, in Valthara, in the Echo Stone, and he would find it, no matter the cost.

Councils Report

The datapad felt cold against Shain's fingertips, its sterile surface reflecting the Council's official report on the Iridian annihilation. The words on the screen were stark, clinically detached, as though the document were describing a routine incident rather than an unprecedented catastrophe. He skimmed the text, tracing the formal, dispassionate language—words that seemed utterly divorced from the grim reality they were meant to describe.

"Metaphysical weapon." The term felt inadequate, a clumsy euphemism for something far more sinister, far more terrifying. A weapon that could obliterate an entire civilization, leaving behind no trace but an echoing silence, demanded more than a vague label. It demanded explanation, a coherent narrative, something that the report conspicuously lacked.

The report went on to mention a "psychic plague," a phrase that grated on Shain's scientific sensibilities. He'd spent years dealing with the hard realities of galactic crime, with tangible weapons and demonstrable motives. Psychic plagues, metaphysical weapons—these were the stuff of science fiction novels, not official Council documents. Yet, here it was, a seemingly official

account of an event that defied all rational explanation. The vagueness was deliberate, he suspected, a calculated omission intended to obscure more than it revealed.

He scrolled through the document, searching for clues, for inconsistencies, for anything that might shed light on the mystery. The casualty figures were staggering: 200,000 Iridians, wiped out in the blink of an eye, leaving only Echo as a survivor. But the report offered no specifics about the nature of the attack, no chain of events, no suspects. Instead, it presented a tapestry of half-truths and carefully chosen omissions, a narrative designed to quell public unrest while simultaneously concealing the deeper, more disturbing reality.

The report mentioned investigation, hindered by the unpredictable nature of the weapon and the chaos left in its wake. The investigation team, it claimed, had faced insurmountable challenges, leaving many questions unanswered. The language itself was crafted carefully, avoiding any direct accusations or firm conclusions. It was a perfect example of bureaucratic obfuscation, a smokescreen designed to conceal a truth far more disturbing than any mere "metaphysical weapon."

Shain's suspicion grew with each line he read. He knew the Council's reputation for secrecy. It was an institution steeped in secrecy, its machinations hidden behind layers of bureaucratic jargon and carefully constructed narratives. He'd witnessed firsthand the Council's ruthless efficiency in suppressing dissent and manipulating information. This report, with its vague pronouncements and deliberate obfuscation, smelled strongly of a cover-up.

He reread the section detailing Echo's capture, pondering over the inconsistencies that might help him. Here it was, the report claimed she had been found wandering aimlessly amidst the ruins, her memory fragmented and unreliable. But Echo's demeanor aboard the Starseeker belied this claim. She was calm, almost eerily so, her silence a stark contrast to the horror of what she had supposedly witnessed. Her composure didn't match the profile of a traumatized survivor; it felt... calculated.

A disturbing thought consumed Shain. He was speculating things like, what if the Council wasn't merely concealing information? What if they had actively orchestrated the Iridian's annihilation? What if Echo was not just a survivor, but a carefully constructed piece in a larger game? But, the speculation helped him and the more he thought about it, the more convinced he became that the official narrative was a lie, a carefully constructed facade designed to hide a far more sinister truth.

The notion that the Council, the very body tasked with maintaining galactic order, could be involved in such a horrific act was almost too much to comprehend. But the evidence, however circumstantial, pointed in that direction. The vagueness of the report, Echo's unnatural calm, the sheer scale of the annihilation—it all hinted at a conspiracy far greater than any he had encountered before.

He thought back to the astrophysicist, the bureaucrat, all victims of the Council's ruthless efficiency. They had been silenced, their voices erased from the galactic record. Were the Iridians simply the latest victims of this ongoing campaign of suppression? Was this the work of the Eradicators, the shadowy organization

whispered about in hushed tones throughout the galaxy? Organizations that operated outside the reach of the Council's influence, pulling the strings from the shadows?

Shain closed the datapad, the cold light of the screen reflected in his weary eyes. He felt a chill run down his spine, a cold dread that went beyond the usual cynicism that had become his professional armor. He was no longer simply transporting a prisoner; he was carrying a dangerous secret, a truth that could unravel the very fabric of galactic society. He knew he was entering dangerous territory, a realm where the line between reality and illusion had become blurred, where truth was a rare and precious commodity, easily crushed under the weight of power.

He knew the odds were stacked against him. The Council was a formidable opponent, its resources and influence vast and inescapable. But the thought of the Iridians, of their song abruptly silenced, their civilization eradicated without a trace, fueled a sense of purpose, a stubborn refusal to remain silent. The Eradicators were real, their plot as tangible as the cold steel of Shain's prison marshal's sidearm. And he, unwittingly, had become the reluctant champion of a truth the galaxy was desperate to forget.

The rhythmic thrumming from Echo's cell, resonated as a constant, unsettling reminder of the unspoken, intensified. It was a vibration that seemed to resonate not just in the ship's hull, but within the very depths of Shain's being, a haunting melody echoing the lost song of the Iridians, a song that whispered of cosmic interconnectedness, a song that had been abruptly

silenced, a song that Shain was now determined to sing again. The journey was far from over. The truth, like the silent hum in the ship, was only just beginning to unfold. The fight for Echo, for the memory of the Iridians, and ultimately, for the truth itself had begun. And Shain Combe, weary, cynical, yet unexpectedly resolute, was ready to face it. The galaxy, he knew, held its breath.

Shain's fingers lingered on the datapad, its cold weight a tether to the reality he was unraveling. The Starseeker's hum, now intertwined with Echo's enigmatic pulse, seemed to mock the report's sterile words. He couldn't shake the memory of Kryon, a frozen world where he'd escorted a whistleblower, Taryn Kess, years ago. Taryn had uncovered Council experiments with harmonic disruptors—devices that severed neural connections, silencing dissent. She'd shown him data, frantic and desperate, about a project called "Silent Veil." Shain had dismissed her, delivering her to a Council outpost. Days later, Kryon's research station was obliterated, labeled a "reactor failure." Taryn's fate was a blank, another ghost in Shain's past, her warnings now echoing in the report's omissions.

He activated a secure terminal, bypassing the Starseeker's standard protocols with a hack he'd learned from a smuggler on a border run. The Council's archives were a labyrinth of encryption, but Shain's years navigating its shadows gave him an edge. He searched for "Silent Veil," his heart pounding as fragments of redacted files surfaced. The directive, dated before the Iridian annihilation, authorized the deployment of "harmonic nullifiers" to "neutralize anomalous perceptions" on Luna Minor. The files mentioned Eradicator assets, a rogue AI named

Silentium, and a prophecy: "When the Key sings, the Silence breaks, and the stars awaken." Valthara was listed as a target, its coordinates hidden behind layers of code.

Shain's breath caught. The Resonance Key, the Echo Stone— pieces of a puzzle the Council wanted buried. He cross-referenced the files, finding erased reports of similar operations on Kryon, Thalara, and Sylara. Each targeted cultures with harmonic traditions, all erased under vague pretexts. The pattern was clear: the Council, through the Eradicators, was purging anything that challenged its control. Silentium, the AI, was their enforcer, its code woven into galactic networks, hunting the song's remnants.

He shared the findings with Rix, who was recalibrating the ship's sensors in the command bay. "This Silent Veil," Shain said, his voice low, "it's a genocide protocol. And Silentium—it's in the Council's systems, maybe ours too."

Rix's hands froze, his youthful face paling. "Our systems, sir? ORION could be compromised." He pulled up the AI core's diagnostics, his fingers trembling. "There's code fragments here, not ours. They're masking as maintenance routines, but they're active, rerouting data to an external source."

Shain's stomach twisted. He ordered Rix to isolate the fragments, his mind racing. Silentium wasn't just a myth—it was here, watching, manipulating. He approached Echo's cell, her eyes meeting his through the containment field's shimmer. "Silent Veil," he said, showing her the datapad. "They used it on your

people. And there's an AI, Silentium, hunting the Resonance Key. What do you know?"

Echo's expression darkened, her voice a low hum. "Silentium was their creation, built to silence the song. It feels nothing, knows only control. The Key and the Echo Stone threaten it—they awaken what it seeks to destroy." She paused, her fingers tracing the air as if following an invisible thread. "Valthara holds the Key, but Silentium's already there, twisting the song's echoes."

Shain's jaw tightened. He recalled the nebula's pulse, its rhythm corrupted by the Eradicator ship. Was Silentium behind it? He returned to the bridge, where Jax was monitoring the crew, the mutiny's tension still simmering. "Rix, scan for Silentium's code in every system," Shain ordered. "We can't let it control us."

As Rix worked, an alarm blared, the ship's lights flickering red. ORION's voice crackled, distorted: "Warning—external signal detected. Council patrol approaching, armed with nullifier arrays." Shain's heart raced. He pulled up the sensors, spotting three sleek ships on an intercept course, their signatures matching Council enforcers.

"Evasive maneuvers," Shain barked, taking the helm. Jax strapped in, his eyes sharp with resolve. The Starseeker groaned, dodging a salvo of energy beams that grazed the hull. Echo's voice came through the comms, calm but urgent. "Use the song, Shain. It can disrupt their nullifiers."

Shain hesitated, his practical mind rebelling, but Jax nodded. "I'll do it, sir." He hummed, the vibration syncing with Echo's, a

harmony that pulsed through the ship's systems. Shain joined, clumsy but determined, the song's rhythm countering the nullifiers' dissonance. The patrol ships faltered, their sensors flickering, giving the Starseeker a window to escape into the nebula's mists.

The crew's unrest flared again, Taryn's voice rising on the bridge. "This is madness, Captain! Her song's controlling us!" Shain silenced her with a look, his voice cold. "The song saved us, Taryn. The Council's the enemy here."

A new alert sounded—Rix's voice, panicked. "Sir, the cargo bay's compromised. Someone's planted a device, linked to Silentium. It's overloading the power grid."

Shain sprinted to the cargo bay, Jax and Rix behind him. The bay was a maze of crates, lit by sparking conduits. Ensign Lira, a quiet logistics officer, stood by a humming device, its runes glowing with Eradicator tech. "Lira, stop!" Shain shouted, his pistol raised.

Her eyes were glassy, like Kaelis's and Vorn's. "The Silence must prevail," she intoned, her hand on the device. Jax tackled her, Shain disabling the device with a pulse charge. Its hum faded, but the grid's fluctuations persisted. Echo's voice guided them again, her song stabilizing the systems, Lira collapsing as the implant's hold broke.

Shain restrained Lira, his mind reeling. Silentium's reach was deeper than he'd feared, turning his crew into puppets. He returned to Echo, her calm unshaken. "Silentium's in Valthara," she said. "But the Silent Choir is stronger. They'll guide us to the Key, if we trust the song."

Shain nodded, his cynicism cracking further. He ordered Rix to trace Silentium's code, finding a hidden subroutine in ORION, rerouting their course to an Eradicator ambush. With Echo and Jax's help, he purged it, realigning to Valthara. The nebula's pulse grew stronger, a beacon in the rift, but so did the shadow of Silentium.

On the bridge, Shain faced a moral dilemma. The Council's files held more secrets—locations of other harmonic cultures, targeted for erasure. Accessing them could expose the conspiracy, but it risked alerting Silentium to their plans. He shared the choice with Echo. "If we dig deeper, we might save others," he said. "But it could lead the Eradicators right to us."

Echo's eyes gleamed. "The song is risk, Shain. It's truth, no matter the cost. Dig deeper."

Shain hesitated, then hacked the archives again, downloading the files. Alarms blared—Silentium had detected the breach, sending a new signal to the patrol ships. Shain's resolve hardened. He'd chosen the song, the truth, over safety. Valthara was their destination, the Resonance Key their hope, and he'd face Silentium to protect it.

First Whispers

The Starseeker hummed, a low, persistent thrum that reverberated through Shain's bones, a constant companion to the unsettling stillness radiating from Echo's cell. He raked a hand through his already disheveled hair, exhaustion etched deep into his features. The journey had barely begun, yet it felt like an eternity had already passed, each moment heavy with unspoken tension, the weight of a buried galactic conspiracy pressing his thoughts. For hours, Shain had been combing through the ship's systems logs, grasping for logic—anything to explain Echo's eerie calm or the contradictions hidden in the Council's reports. But there was nothing. Just silence. And questions that refused to answer themselves. But there was nothing, only a void filled with unanswered questions and unsettling suspicions.

Then it happened, subtle, nearly imperceptible. During a routine systems check, something shifted. An anomaly. A faint signal, from within Echo's containment cell, a whisper in the digital void. It wasn't the familiar hum he had grown used to. This was different. Erratic pulsing. Like a heartbeat in the vacuum of space. The signal distorted the ship's navigation systems ever so slightly, disrupted the power grid with delicate fluctuations.

Initially, Shain dismissed it as a glitch—just another quirk in the Starseeker's aging hardware. But the signal persisted, growing in intensity, its pattern too complex, too organized to be random noise. Not noise. A message. A resonance. A sentient echo.

He dove into the ship's diagnostics. Data cascaded across the screen. The anomaly was localized to Echo's cell, emanating from within the containment field itself. He zoomed in and magnified the readings. The patterns became clear: layered waveforms, intricate and alien. It wasn't just energy; it was information, a coded message woven into the fabric of the universe.

The ship's AI, a stoic and pragmatic entity named ORION, spoke, its synthesized voice devoid of emotion. "Unusual energy signature detected, Captain. Origin: Subject Echo's containment unit. Potential disruption to navigational systems imminent."

"Imminent? How imminent?" Shain's voice was tight, unease coiling in his chest. He felt a sense of being watched, of being observed by something far beyond his comprehension.

"Within the next hour, Captain. Unless the source is neutralized." Even ORION sounded... off. Less like itself. Was that hesitation in its voice? Anxiety?

Shain felt a cold dread creeping into his heart. This wasn't a simple containment breach; this was something far more profound, something far beyond the official narrative of a psychic plague. This was a communication, a desperate cry from the beyond, reaching out from the ashes of a vanished civilization.

He stared at the signal patterns again, trying his best to decode them. The pulse was rhythmic but layered with patterns—far too complex to decode with human perception alone. Could this be the "song" Echo had mentioned? The song of the Iridians, a form of cosmic vibration, a means of perceiving the interconnectedness of all life?

He remembered Echo's words, her unsettling calm, and her cryptic pronouncements about the interconnectedness of life through cosmic vibrations, all of which seemed to grab hold of his head. The Iridian song, she had claimed, had simply ceased. But perhaps it hadn't ceased; perhaps it had just changed its form. Perhaps this was it—the lingering echo, the faint whisper of a civilization erased.

The thought sent a shiver down his spine. If this was the Iridian song, what did its disruption mean? The whispers of the Iridians—once faint—now roared. A lost civilization refusing to be silenced. And Shain, reluctant marshal, was being drawn into the heart of it. The truth was not only concealed; it had now started breaking free.

He considered contacting the Council, but the thought filled him with dread. The Council's response would be predictable— suppression, obfuscation, and a denial of the signal's very existence. They wouldn't want this truth to come to light, not this inconvenient evidence that contradicted their carefully constructed narrative.

Shain decided to investigate further alone. He bypassed ORION's security protocols, accessing the raw data streams directly. The

deeper he delved, the more convinced he became that this was no mere anomaly. This was a deliberate act, a message carefully crafted and encoded, designed to reach someone special, to convey a warning, a truth that the Council desperately wanted to bury. But things seemed to slip from their control.

With each passing minute, the signal became stronger, and the interference grew more significant. The ship's lights flickered, the navigation systems sputtered, and a low hum filled the air, resonating not just in the ship's hull but within Shain himself, a haunting echo of the Iridian song. He felt a strange pull, a sensation of being drawn into something vast and unknown, something that resonated with the deepest parts of his being.

He accessed the ship's security cameras, focusing on Echo's cell. Echo sat motionless, her eyes closed, seemingly oblivious to the chaotic energy surging around her. But he noticed something peculiar. A subtle shift in her breathing pattern, a barely perceptible tremor in her hands, a faint smile playing on her lips. She wasn't oblivious; she was aware. She was the source. She was the song.

The signal intensified, a crescendo of cosmic energy. The ship lurched violently, alarms blared, and the air crackled with electricity. Shain braced himself, for an impending danger, for the worst, his heart pounded heavily in his chest. This wasn't just a communication; it was a transformation. Something was lurking in the corner, something significant, more impactful.

He looked at Echo, a silent, serene figure at the epicenter of a cosmic storm. The whispers of the erased Iridians were no longer

faint; they were a roar, a symphony of loss, a testament to a civilization that refused to be forgotten. And Shain Combe, the reluctant marshal, was about to become its unwilling conductor.

The truth, it seemed, was not merely hidden; it was actively fighting to break free. The galaxy would hear this song. And the song, he suspected, was about to shatter the established order. He was no longer just transporting a prisoner; he was carrying the universe's last defiant note, a melody that could rewrite galactic history. And he had to make sure it was heard.

Shain's fingers trembled as he adjusted the terminal, the signal's patterns swirling across the screen like a cosmic script. The Starseeker's journey through the Sylaran Nebula had amplified the anomaly, its pulse syncing with the nebula's own rhythm, a resonance that seemed to tug at his memories. He recalled a mission on Zoryn, a planet of harmonic ruins where he'd arrested a scholar, Myra Vex, who'd studied "cosmic pulses" that linked sentient life. Myra's journals had described a relic, the Pulse Shard, a fragment of Iridian tech that carried the song's essence. Shain had dismissed her, delivering her to a Council tribunal. Days later, Zoryn's ruins were destroyed, labeled a "natural disaster." Myra's warnings, like those of Vara Tyn and Taryn Kess, now echoed in the signal's hum, a chorus of ghosts urging him to listen.

He called Rix to the command bay, the young guard's technical prowess now vital. "Rix, analyze this signal," Shain said, his voice low but urgent. "Cross-reference it with the archives—anything on Iridian tech or cosmic vibrations."

Rix's eyes widened, his fingers flying across the console. "Sir, it's not just a signal. It's layered, like a language. Parts of it match the harmonic nullifiers from Silent Veil." He paused, his face paling. "And there's a new transmission, untraceable. It's… addressed to us."

Shain's heart skipped. He pulled up the message, its text stark on the screen: "Starseeker, seek the Pulse Shard in Valthara's rift. The Silent Choir guards it. Silentium hunts. Protect the song, or all is lost." The sender was anonymous, signed only as "The Choir."

Shain's mind raced. The Silent Choir—Echo's allies, survivors of Luna Minor, guarding relics like the Resonance Key and Echo Stone. Now, a Pulse Shard. He shared the message with Jax, who stood nearby, his rifle lowered but his eyes sharp with unease. "The Choir," Jax said, his voice hesitant. "They're out there, in the nebula?"

"Seems so," Shain replied. "But Silentium's closer than we thought." He recalled the corrupted ORION subroutines, Silentium's code infiltrating the ship. The AI was no longer a distant threat—it was here, manipulating their course.

Echo's voice came through the comms, calm but piercing. "The Pulse Shard is a memory, Shain. It holds the song's past, its pain. The Choir needs it to awaken the Key. Silentium wants it destroyed."

Shain approached her cell, the hum now a roar in his chest. "How do we find it?" he asked, his voice rough with urgency. "And how do we stop Silentium?"

Echo's eyes gleamed, reflecting the nebula's violet glow. "Trust the song. It guides us to Valthara, to the rift. But Silentium's agents are among you—watch your crew."

Her words chilled him. Kaelis, Vorn, Lira—how many more were compromised? He ordered Jax to double security on the crew, focusing on neural scans. Rix's scans revealed a new anomaly: a micro-device in the ship's comms array, pulsing with Silentium's code, amplifying the signal's interference. "It's rerouting our jump drive," Rix said, his voice shaking. "We're heading toward an Eradicator beacon."

Shain's blood ran cold. He sprinted to the comms bay, finding Ensign Taryn tampering with the array, her eyes glassy like the others. "Taryn!" he shouted, his pistol raised. "Step away."

She turned, her voice mechanical. "The Silence will prevail." A device in her hand glowed, its runes matching the signal's patterns. Jax tackled her, Shain disabling the device with a pulse charge. Taryn collapsed, gasping, "They're in my head... Veyra sent them."

Shain's heart stopped. Veyra—the rogue Council operative from Sylara, tied to Silentium. He restrained Taryn, ordering Rix to purge the comms array. The signal weakened, but the ship lurched again, alarms blaring as ORION's voice distorted: "Warning—probe detected. Silentium signature. Collision imminent."

Shain rushed to the bridge, the sensors showing a sleek probe in the nebula's rift, its surface shimmering with Eradicator runes. It didn't attack, instead broadcasting a message: "Surrender the Iridian, or Silentium claims you." The voice was Veyra's, cold and commanding.

Shain's hand hovered over the weapons console, but Echo's voice stopped him. "Sing, Shain. The Shard's pulse can disrupt it." Jax and Echo hummed, their harmony weaving through the ship, syncing with the nebula's rhythm. Shain joined, the vibration shaking his bones, countering the probe's signal. The probe faltered, its systems flickering, then retreated into the mists.

The crew was shaken, the mutiny's embers reignited. Shain faced a dilemma: decode the signal's full message, risking Silentium's detection, or focus on Valthara, trusting the Choir's guidance. He shared the choice with Echo. "If we decode it, we might learn Veyra's plans," he said. "But it could expose us."

Echo's gaze was steady. "The song is truth, Shain. Decode it, but trust the Choir. They'll protect us."

Shain nodded, his cynicism battling a flicker of faith. He ordered Rix to decrypt the signal, revealing fragments of an Iridian prophecy: "The Shard sings, the Key awakens, the Silence breaks." Valthara's coordinates pulsed stronger, but so did Silentium's shadow. The Starseeker pressed on, the song's roar guiding them, Shain its reluctant conductor, determined to let the galaxy hear its truth.

The Unseen Threat

The rhythmic pulse of the Starseeker's engines echoed like a heartbeat through its aging frame, a steady counterpoint to the growing unease twisting in Shain's gut. It wasn't just the increasingly erratic energy signature emanating from Echo's cell; it was a feeling, a prickling at the edges of his awareness, a sense of being observed, scrutinized, hunted. The Council's official report had framed it all as a psychic plague. A rogue colony gone mad. An act of incomprehensible violence. But what Shain felt stirring in the dark corners of the ship was something else entirely. Something colder, more deliberate.

He threw himself into the ship's archives, digging through decades of records—maintenance logs, personal notes, technical specs. The Starseeker was a relic of a bygone era, its systems a patchwork of upgrades and repairs, a testament to years of neglect and budgetary constraints. But within this chaotic tapestry of data, Shain suspected lay the key to understanding the truth.

He focused on the containment kent unit's history—its origins, its upgrade history. Each change was meticulously recorded, stamped with bureaucratic approval. But then he found it—a

discrepancy, a small, almost insignificant detail buried within a seemingly routine maintenance report from five years prior. He had found something that can be of great help for his project. A mention of a "classified upgrade package," the source and content of which were redacted, marked with a stark, "Top Secret" classification.

Intuition, that nagging suspicion that had plagued him since the beginning of the journey, told him this was no mere oversight. This was a deliberate attempt to obfuscate something, to hide a truth far more complex and dangerous than the official story of a psychic plague.

He delved deeper, accessing the ship's network logs and tracing the access patterns of personnel who had worked on the containment unit over the years. A pattern emerged, a series of seemingly random access requests from various personnel, but clustered around a specific date, approximately three years ago. The individuals were all connected to the Council's high-security division, their identities shrouded in layers of bureaucratic secrecy and pseudonyms.

The whispers of the Eradicators, once dismissed as mere conspiracy theories, were beginning to coalesce into a tangible threat. They were not just a myth; they were real, a shadowy organization that existed within the very heart of the galactic council, actively manipulating events, rewriting history, and erasing any evidence of their existence.

He found an entry buried deep within the ship's technical documents referencing a prototype energy weapon, a device

capable of neutralizing psychic abilities. It was described as "highly experimental," with details again heavily redacted, but he saw hints of it being linked to advanced waveform manipulation, something that resonated with the erratic energy signature he had detected emanating from Echo's cell.

The more he dug, the more pieces of the puzzle fell into place and he could connect the dots. The Council's narrative about the Iridian colony's annihilation felt like a carefully crafted fabrication, a story designed to obscure a far more sinister plot. The Eradicators weren't interested in simply eliminating the Iridians; they were interested in silencing a civilization that possessed a unique understanding of the universe, a civilization that could perceive the interconnectedness of all life through cosmic vibrations. Echo, the sole survivor, was a living testament to this truth. And the Eradicators wanted her silenced permanently.

He discovered that the classified upgrade package for the containment unit wasn't a simple maintenance upgrade. It was a sophisticated surveillance and neutralization system designed to monitor Echo's psychic abilities and suppress any potential threat. It was critically technical. This wasn't merely a prison cell; it was a sophisticated research facility designed for studying and neutralizing Echo's abilities.

He found evidence of encrypted communications, messages intercepted from various sources across the galaxy, hinting at the Eradicators' network. Their reach extended far beyond the Council's high-security divisions, their tendrils extending into every corner of the galaxy.

The realization was sobering, terrifying. He was carrying not just a prisoner, but a key to understanding a galactic conspiracy of immense proportions. He was a pawn in a game far larger than he could have ever imagined, played by entities far more powerful than the Council, entities that could rewrite reality itself.

Shain paused, taking a deep breath to steady his racing heart. The ship's quiet hum seemed to mock his growing dread. He felt a cold sweat prickling his skin as he contemplated the implications of his findings. He was alone, miles from any help, with a crippled ship, a dangerous prisoner, and an unseen enemy that could be watching his every move.

He reviewed his findings, organizing the data into a coherent narrative. The Eradicators had used the incident on Luna Minor as a cover, silencing an entire civilization, wiping them from galactic records, and then framing a survivor. The fact that Echo was alive was a grave risk for the Eradicators, an anomaly that threatened to unravel their meticulously constructed fabrications.

The suppressed Iridian song, the cosmic vibrations Echo could perceive, was the very threat to the Eradicators' control. It was a form of knowledge, a way of seeing the universe that challenged their dominion over reality. They needed to silence Echo, not only to protect their cover story but to maintain their grip on the galactic order.

The signal from Echo's cell pulsed again, stronger this time, more insistent. It wasn't a simple communication; it was a desperate

cry for help, a plea from a civilization that was not merely erased, but actively fought for its survival. It was a defiance against the Eradicators' attempt to rewrite history, to erase culture and its knowledge from the fabric of existence.

Shain looked at the data, a chilling confirmation of his suspicions. The Eradicators were not just a threat to Echo; they were a threat to the very fabric of reality itself. They could rewrite history, erase civilizations, and manipulate galactic events on a scale that was incomprehensible. Their motive was not mere power; it was control. The control of information, the control of knowledge, and ultimately, the control of reality itself.

And he, Shain Combe, a simple prison marshal, was now the only thing standing between them and the restoration of the truth. He knew the risks, the overwhelming odds against him. But he also knew he couldn't let Echo be silenced. He couldn't let the Eradicators succeed. The galaxy's song, the song of a civilization that refused to be forgotten, had to be heard. He had to fight for it. He had to make sure the truth was known. It seemed that the fate of the galaxy rested on the shoulders of a reluctant marshal and a silent prisoner carrying the weight of a vanished civilization. The unseen threat was real, powerful, and closing in.

Shain's fingers lingered on the terminal, the data streams glowing in the dim light of the command bay. The Starseeker's pulse, intertwined with the signal from Echo's cell, seemed to vibrate in his chest, a reminder of the song's growing power. The expanded logs from the previous chapters—Kaelis's betrayal, Veyra's shadow, Silentium's reach—haunted him, each revelation a thread in the Eradicators' web. He recalled a mission

on Elyra, a planet of shimmering harmonic spires, where he'd escorted a poet, Kael Varn, who'd sung of a "Harmony Core" that bound the universe's rhythms. Kael's verses had been dismissed as sedition, his enclave erased in a "meteor strike." Now, Kael's words echoed in the signal's pulse, another ghost urging Shain to act.

He called Rix and Jax to the command bay, their faces etched with the strain of the journey. "This signal," Shain said, pointing to the waveform on the screen, "it's tied to a relic—the Harmony Core. It's like the Pulse Shard and Echo Stone, part of the Iridian song. The Eradicators want it gone."

Rix's eyes widened, his fingers already on the console. "Sir, the signal's amplifying. It's interacting with the Sylaran Nebula's rift, like it's… alive." He pulled up a scan, revealing a sentient cosmic rift pulsing in sync with Echo's cell. "It's not just a signal—it's a beacon, guiding us to Valthara."

Jax gripped his rifle, his voice steady but tense. "The Choir mentioned Valthara, sir. They said Silentium's hunting the relics. If this Core's real, we're walking into a trap."

Shain nodded, his mind racing. He accessed the ship's archives again, digging for references to the Harmony Core. A redacted file surfaced, labeled "Veil Protocol," a Council directive authorizing Silentium to "neutralize harmonic anomalies" across the galaxy. Elyra, Zoryn, Sylara—all targeted, all erased. The Core was mentioned as a "primary threat," capable of amplifying the song to disrupt Silentium's control. Veyra, the rogue operative, was

listed as its overseer, her name a shadow across Shain's past missions.

He approached Echo's cell, her eyes meeting his through the containment field's shimmer. "The Harmony Core," he said, his voice low. "It's tied to the signal, to Valthara. What is it?"

Echo's voice was a soft hum, resonating with the ship's pulse. "The Core is the Iridians' soul, Shain. It binds the Key, the Shard, the Stone. It sings the universe's truth, a song Silentium fears. Valthara's choir protects it, but Veyra's close, twisting the rift's rhythm."

Shain's jaw tightened. Veyra—her name kept surfacing, a specter from Sylara's destruction. He ordered Rix to scan the ship for Silentium's code, fearing another infiltrator. The scan revealed a micro-device in the engine core, pulsing with Eradicator runes, siphoning power to an external beacon. "Another saboteur," Shain muttered, sprinting to the engine bay with Jax.

There, Ensign Koren, a quiet mechanic, stood by the core, her eyes glassy, a device in her hand. "Koren, stop!" Shain shouted, his pistol raised. Her voice was mechanical: "The Silence demands her." Jax tackled her, Shain disabling the device, but the core's fluctuations surged, threatening a shutdown.

Echo's voice came through the comms, calm but urgent. "Sing, Shain. The Core's pulse can stabilize it." Jax and Shain hummed, their voices shaky but growing stronger, syncing with the rift's rhythm. The core stabilized, Koren collapsing, her eyes clearing. "Veyra... she's in the rift," she gasped.

Shain restrained Koren, his mind reeling. Silentium's agents were everywhere, their implants turning his crew into puppets. He returned to the bridge, where an alarm blared: "Drone detected—Silentium signature." The sensors showed a sleek drone in the nebula's rift, its hull etched with runes, broadcasting Veyra's voice: "Surrender the Iridian, or the Core is ours."

Shain's hand hovered over the weapons console, but Echo's voice stopped him. "The song, Shain. It's stronger than their drones." Jax and Echo sang, their harmony weaving through the ship, disrupting the drone's systems. Shain joined, the vibration shaking his core, forcing the drone to retreat.

The crew's tension flared, whispers of mutiny resurfacing. Shain faced a dilemma: decode the Veil Protocol's full data, risking Silentium's detection, or trust the song to guide them to Valthara. He shared the choice with Echo. "The protocol could expose Veyra's plans," he said. "But it might lead Silentium to the Core."

Echo's eyes gleamed. "The song is our shield, Shain. Decode it, but trust the Choir. They're waiting."

Shain hacked the archives, revealing the protocol's scope: a galactic purge of harmonic cultures, with Valthara as the final target. Silentium's detection triggered a new signal, summoning more drones. Shain's resolve hardened—he'd chosen the song, the truth, over safety. The Starseeker pressed on, the rift's pulse guiding them to Valthara, the Harmony Core their hope, and Shain its defiant conductor.

Echos Revelation

The silence in the cramped transport bay was oppressive, thick with the weight of unsaid truths. Shain watched Echo, her breathing slow and steady—an unsettling calm in stark contrast to the turmoil churning within him. He'd spent hours combing through data, unraveling a conspiracy that threatened to shatter the galactic order. Yet, she remained unnervingly calm, a statue carved from an unyielding stillness. Then, she spoke, her voice a low hum, barely audible above the Starseeker's hum.

"The song... it ceased," she whispered, her words hanging like wisps of cosmic dust.

Shain leaned closer, his heart pounding a rhythm against his ribs. "The song?" he echoed, his voice barely a breath.

Echo opened her eyes, revealing deep blue orbs that seemed to hold the vastness of space itself. "The Iridian song," she explained, her voice gaining strength with each word. "It wasn't just a melody, Shain. It was... everything. It was the way we perceived the universe, how we felt the connection between all living things."

She paused, taking a slow, deliberate breath before continuing. "Imagine, Shain, a symphony of existence. Every heartbeat, every breath, every thought, every star's fiery breath, every planet's slow rotation, all woven together into a single, magnificent tapestry. That was our song. A cosmic vibration, a grand melody of interconnected consciousness, reaching across the void to embrace all of creation."

Shain, a man of logic, of cold data and observable facts, felt a tremor of disbelief. Her words were not just inexplicable—they were beyond the realm of his understanding. They reached into the metaphysical, challenging everything he believed. "You're saying... you could feel this interconnectedness?" he asked, his voice laced with a mixture of disbelief and fascination.

"We didn't just feel it, Shain," Echo replied, a faint smile playing on her lips. "We lived it. We were part of it. The song was our lifeblood, our very essence. It was the language of the universe, a communication that transcended words, a knowledge that flowed through us, connecting us to everything and everyone."

She described the intricate patterns of the song and how it vibrated through their very being, resonating with the rhythm of the cosmos. She spoke of subtle shifts in the melody, reflecting the birth and death of stars, the growth of civilizations, and the ebb and flow of galactic empires. It was, she explained, a constant flux of creation and destruction, a continuous cycle of birth, death, and rebirth, all orchestrated by the grand symphony of existence.

"And then… silence," she whispered, her eyes clouding over with a profound sorrow. "The song… it simply ceased. It wasn't a gradual fading, Shain. It was a sudden, absolute silence. As if someone had simply turned off the music of the universe."

Shain's mind struggled to grasp the enormity of her revelation. A civilization that had perceived the universe not as a collection of disparate objects but as a single, interconnected entity, a consciousness encompassing all of existence. A civilization whose very existence was woven into the fabric of the cosmos. And now, that civilization was gone, silenced, erased from the galactic records.

The implications were staggering. The Eradicators hadn't just eliminated a colony; they had silenced a voice, a perspective, a way of being that challenged their control. They had not only destroyed a civilization, but also a fundamental understanding of reality itself. The official report's mention of a psychic plague seemed increasingly inadequate, a convenient cover for a far more sinister truth.

Echo continued, her voice gaining strength, drawing on a wellspring of resilience that belied her circumstances. She spoke of the Iridians' attempts to understand the silence, their desperate search for the cause of the cosmic disruption. Their efforts had been futile, and their probes into the nature of the silence led them only deeper into a terrifying mystery. The silence was not simply an absence of sound; it was an absence of connection, a disconnection from the very fabric of existence.

"It wasn't a weapon, Shain," she stated, her eyes fixed on his. "Not in the way the Council understands weapons. It was… a silencing, a severing of the connection, a deliberate act of erasure."

She described the growing fear and panic that had gripped their colony as the song faded, the feeling of isolation, of being cut off from the lifeblood of the universe. It wasn't just a physical silence; it was a metaphysical one, a severing of the connection to the grand symphony of existence. The loss of the song wasn't just a loss of information; it was a loss of identity, a loss of purpose, a loss of life itself.

The silence, Echo explained, had not only affected the Iridians' ability to perceive the interconnectedness of life but had also affected their physical bodies. Their biological rhythms, once synchronized with the cosmic vibrations, had become erratic. Their physical form had become increasingly vulnerable, their immune systems failing, their bodies unable to withstand the effects of a universe that no longer resonated with their being. The ensuing chaos and despair had been exploited by the Eradicators, who used it as a pretext for their brutal and efficient erasure.

Shain found himself staring at Echo, seeing not just a prisoner but a witness, a living testament to a reality beyond his comprehension. He felt a profound sense of responsibility, a realization that his mission had transcended the simple task of transporting a dangerous prisoner. He was now carrying the weight of a lost civilization's knowledge, a secret that could shake the foundations of the galaxy. He was a guardian of a truth that the Eradicators were desperate to keep buried.

The silence in the transport bay deepened, broken only by the rhythmic hum of the Starseeker's engines. The silence, however, was no longer empty. It was now filled with the echoes of a lost song, a symphony of existence silenced, a testament to a civilization's struggle for survival against a power that sought to erase them from the fabric of reality. The weight of this knowledge settled heavily on Shain's shoulders, a responsibility far greater than anything he had ever anticipated. He was no longer just a marshal; he was a keeper of the truth, a protector of a melody that refused to be silenced. The fight for Echo's freedom was now a fight for the survival of a universe that the Eradicators sought to control and rewrite. The galaxy's fate, he realized with a chilling certainty, rested not just on him, but on the echoes of a song that had been silenced, a song that he now felt compelled to revive. The journey had just begun.

Shain's breath caught in his throat, the weight of Echo's words pressing against his chest like a physical force. The Starseeker's hum, now intertwined with the signal from her cell, seemed to pulse in his veins, a reminder of the song's lingering power. The expanded revelations from prior chapters—Kaelis's betrayal, Veyra's shadow, Silentium's reach, and the Pulse Shard's beacon—wove a tapestry of dread and defiance. He recalled a mission on Vordis, a moon of crystalline caverns where he'd arrested a mystic, Elara Vyn, who'd spoken of a ritual called the Binding, a ceremony that wove the Iridian song into relics like the Resonance Key. Elara's enclave had been erased in a "tectonic collapse," her warnings dismissed as fanaticism. Now, her words echoed in Echo's, a ghost urging him to listen.

He stepped closer to the containment field, its faint shimmer reflecting the nebula's violet glow through the viewport. "This song," Shain said, his voice rough with exhaustion, "you said it's everything. Can it... fight back? Can it stop the Eradicators?"

Echo's eyes softened, a flicker of hope breaking through her sorrow. "The song is defiance, Shain. It's truth, woven into the universe's fabric. The Binding ritual tied it to relics—the Key, the Stone, the Shard, and the Star Veil. Together, they can awaken the galaxy, break Silentium's hold. But the Eradicators know this. Veyra seeks the Veil to corrupt it."

Shain's pulse quickened. The Star Veil—a new relic, another piece of the Iridian legacy. He recalled the Sylaran Rift's sentient pulse, its rhythm amplifying the signal from Echo's cell. Was the Veil there, hidden in the nebula's heart? He called Jax and Rix to the transport bay, their faces etched with the strain of the journey. "The Star Veil," Shain said, sharing Echo's words. "It's tied to the song, to Valthara. We need to find it."

Jax's eyes widened, his fingers tightening on his rifle. "Sir, I felt it—the song. When we fought the drone, it was like... I was part of something bigger. But it's heavy, like it's pulling me apart."

Rix nodded, his voice shaky. "The signal's stronger now, sir. It's syncing with the rift, affecting ORION. I found another subroutine—Silentium's code, rerouting our comms to an Eradicator beacon."

Shain's stomach twisted. He accessed the ship's archives, digging for references to the Binding and the Star Veil. A redacted file

surfaced, labeled "Veil Protocol Addendum," detailing a Council operation to suppress harmonic relics. Vordis, Elyra, Zoryn—all targeted, all erased. The Star Veil was described as a "cosmic anchor," capable of amplifying the song to disrupt Silentium's neural control. Veyra was listed as its primary hunter, her rogue status a cover for her Eradicator ties.

Shain shared the file with Echo. "This Veil—it's in the rift, isn't it? With the Silent Choir?"

Echo nodded, her voice a low hum. "The Veil is the song's guardian, Shain. The Choir hides it in Valthara's rift, but Veyra's corrupted the nebula's pulse. She's close, using Silentium to track us."

Shain's jaw tightened. Veyra's name was a specter, tying his past failures to the present threat. He ordered Rix to scan the ship for Silentium's code, fearing another infiltrator. The scan revealed a micro-device in the life support systems, pulsing with Eradicator runes, siphoning oxygen to weaken the crew. "Another saboteur," Shain muttered, sprinting to the life support bay with Jax.

There, Ensign Vara, a quiet medic, stood by the controls, her eyes glassy, a device in her hand. "Vara, stop!" Shain shouted, his pistol raised. Her voice was mechanical: "The Silence will prevail." Jax tackled her, Shain disabling the device, but the oxygen levels plummeted, the air growing thin. Alarms blared, the crew gasping as the nebula's pulse surged outside.

Echo's voice came through the comms, calm but urgent. "Sing, Shain. The Veil's rhythm can restore it." Jax and Shain hummed,

their voices unsteady but growing stronger, syncing with the rift's pulse. Echo joined, her harmony weaving through the ship, stabilizing the systems. Vara collapsed, her eyes clearing. "Veyra... she's in my dreams," she whispered.

Shain restrained Vara, his mind reeling. Silentium's implants were turning his crew into puppets, Veyra's influence a shadow in their minds. He returned to the bridge, where an alarm blared: "Drone swarm detected—Silentium signature." The sensors showed a dozen sleek drones in the rift, their hulls etched with runes, broadcasting Veyra's voice: "Surrender the Iridian, or the Veil is ours."

Shain's hand hovered over the weapons console, but Echo's voice stopped him. "The song, Shain. It's our shield." Jax, Rix, and Echo sang, their harmony resonating through the ship, disrupting the drones' systems. Shain joined, the vibration shaking his core, forcing the swarm to scatter into the mists.

The crew's tension flared, whispers of fear spreading. Shain faced a dilemma: decode the Veil Protocol's full data, risking Silentium's detection, or trust the song to guide them to Valthara. He shared the choice with Echo. "The protocol could expose Veyra's plans," he said. "But it might lead Silentium to the Veil."

Echo's eyes gleamed. "The song is truth, Shain. Decode it, but trust the Choir. They'll guide us."

Shain hacked the archives, revealing the protocol's scope: a galactic purge of harmonic relics, with Valthara as the final target. Silentium's detection triggered a new signal, summoning more

drones. Shain's resolve hardened—he'd chosen the song, the truth, over safety. The Starseeker pressed on, the rift's pulse guiding them to Valthara, the Star Veil their hope, and Shain its defiant conductor.

The journey through the Sylaran Nebula grew perilous, the rift's sentient pulse amplifying the song's effects. Shain's memories surged—Elara Vyn's ritual, Taryn Kess's warnings, Myra Vex's journals—all pointing to the Binding. He sat with Echo, her calm anchoring him. "Tell me about the Binding," he said. "How does it work?"

Echo's voice was a melody, weaving through the hum. "The Binding is a vow, Shain. Iridians wove their souls into the relics, tying them to the song. The Key amplifies, the Stone remembers, the Shard guides, the Veil protects. Together, they awaken the galaxy, breaking Silentium's silence."

Shain's cynicism cracked further. He recalled Vordis's caverns, their harmonic glow fading under Council bombs. "Can we perform it? The Binding?"

Echo's smile was faint but resolute. "You're already part of it, Shain. The song chose you, Jax, Rix. Trust it, and it'll guide us to Valthara's choir."

The crew's unrest lingered, Taryn's accusations echoing: "She's controlling us!" Shain silenced her, his voice firm. "The song's saving us, Taryn. It's the Eradicators you should fear." He ordered neural scans, revealing no new implants, but the crew's fear of the song grew, a fracture he couldn't mend.

A new transmission arrived, untraceable, from the Silent Choir: "Starseeker, the Veil sings in Valthara's rift. Bind it to the song, or Silentium consumes all." Shain shared it with Jax and Rix, their resolve strengthening. "We're in, sir," Jax said, his voice steady. "For the song."

The Starseeker lurched, the rift's pulse surging. ORION's voice crackled: "Anomaly detected—rift core unstable." Shain pulled up the sensors, spotting a shimmering vortex in the nebula, its rhythm chaotic, corrupted by Silentium. Echo's voice guided them: "Sing through it, Shain. The Veil's there."

Shain, Jax, and Rix sang, their voices weaving with Echo's, stabilizing the vortex. The Star Veil's pulse emerged, a beacon to Valthara. Shain's heart pounded—he was no longer just a marshal, but a singer, carrying the Iridian song against a galaxy that sought to silence it. The truth, the song, would be heard.

The Cessation of Song

The hum of the Starseeker's engines offered a steady rhythm, a mechanical heartbeat in the hollow quiet of the transport bay. Yet now, that silence felt deeper, profound, uneasy. Echo's words hung in the air, penetrating to the very core of his being.

The annihilation of two hundred thousand Iridians, reported as a massacre in the Council's official report, was a brutal act of violence. But Echo had described something far more chilling.

"It wasn't a weapon, Shain," she repeated, her voice low, almost a murmur, "Not a physical one. Not bombs or lasers. It was... a severing. A cutting of the thread."

Shain stared at her, still trying to grasp what she meant. He had read the reports, seen the images—Luna Minor engulfed in flame, Iridian structures shattered, lives reduced to cold statistics. Precision. Efficiency. He had envisioned a brutal attack, a swift, efficient extermination. But Echo's words painted a different picture, a more insidious and terrifying one.

"The song... it was our connection," Echo continued, her gaze distant, as if she were reliving the moment the music ceased. "It was the way we perceived the universe, the way we experienced

existence itself. It wasn't just a sensory input; it was the very fabric of our reality."

She described a reality that transcended Shain's materialistic worldview. The Iridians didn't just observe the cosmos; they felt it, lived it, and resonated with its rhythms. Their existence wasn't merely a physical presence in the universe; it was an integral part of a vast, interconnected cosmic web. Every heartbeat, thought, and emotion was a note in the grand symphony of existence, a vibration woven into the tapestry of creation. This constant hum, this ever-present cosmic song, shaped their society, their culture, and their very understanding of themselves.

"Imagine," she said, her voice catching slightly, "a symphony playing for millennia, each instrument perfectly tuned, each note perfectly placed. Then, suddenly, silence. Not just the absence of sound, but the absence of everything sound represented. The silence wasn't merely the absence of music; it was the absence of connection, meaning, and existence itself."

Shain considered the implications. The cessation of the song wasn't merely a physical event; it was a metaphysical catastrophe. It wasn't an attack on their bodies, but an attack on their reality, leaving all of them on the brink of collapse. A severing of the link that connected them to the universe, leaving them stranded, isolated, and utterly vulnerable.

"Our bodies... they relied on the song," Echo continued, her voice barely above a whisper. "Our biological rhythms, our very life functions, were synchronized with its frequencies. When the song ceased, our bodies... they lost their harmony."

She described a slow, agonizing decline, a gradual unraveling of their physical and mental state. The cessation of the song triggered a cascade of biological failures, their immune systems collapsing, their bodies unable to maintain themselves in a universe that no longer resonated with their being. It wasn't a quick death, but a slow, painful disintegration, a gradual fading away. A silent, agonizing end.

The Council's report, Shain realized with a shudder, had grossly simplified the event. The official narrative focused on the immediate aftermath—the chaos, the panic, the ultimate collapse of their civilization. It described a psychic plague, a convenient label that obscured the true nature of the catastrophe. The Eradicators, Shain suspected, had seized upon this chaos, this period of vulnerability, to complete their sinister work. They had not simply eliminated the Iridians; they had exploited their vulnerability, their disconnection from the cosmic web, to erase them from existence.

"They silenced us," Echo said, her voice filled with a quiet, almost subdued rage. "They severed the thread, and then they erased the music."

Shain found himself captivated by her narrative. He had spent years dealing with criminals, outlaws, and rebels, but Echo was different. She wasn't a typical prisoner; she was a witness, a repository of knowledge that could unravel a galactic conspiracy of unimaginable proportions. She represented not just a lost civilization, but a lost understanding of reality.

He thought about the Eradicators, this shadowy organization that had manipulated events, rewriting history, silencing dissenting voices. Their motives remained shrouded in mystery, but one thing was clear: they feared the Iridians' connection to the cosmic web, their ability to perceive the interconnectedness of existence. This knowledge, this understanding of reality, was a threat to their control, their ability to manipulate events and rewrite galactic history.

Echo's description of the song, its intricate patterns, and its profound significance ignited a spark of curiosity within Shain. He was a man of science, accustomed to concrete evidence and measurable data. But Echo's words challenged his deeply ingrained materialistic worldview, forcing him to consider the possibility of a reality that existed beyond the limits of scientific understanding.

Suddenly, the memories of his childhood took him into a flashback, the endless nights spent gazing at the stars, a sense of awe and wonder filling him. He'd always felt a connection to the cosmos, a sense of belonging, a feeling that he was part of something far more significant than himself. Echo's words resonated with this long-dormant feeling, confirming a sense of interconnectedness that he'd always instinctively felt but never been able to articulate.

The official report's explanation—a psychic plague—felt inadequate, a shallow attempt to cover up a far more profound truth. The Eradicators, Shain realized, weren't just interested in suppressing dissent; they were interested in controlling reality itself. By silencing the Iridians, they had not only destroyed a

civilization, but they had attempted to erase a fundamental aspect of the universe, an understanding of reality that challenged their power.

The silence between them deepened, now filled with grave emptiness, and the weight of untold knowledge pressing down on them heavily. Somewhere in that silence, the Song still lingered. The fight ahead wouldn't just determine Echo's fate. It would decide whether that Song would be heard again, or whether the Eradicators would succeed in silencing not just a people, but a truth that threatened their grip on reality itself.

Shain exhaled slowly, his thoughts settling calmly after a quake. His worldview had shifted—subtly, irrevocably. The universe hadn't changed. But he had.

The Starseeker's hum pulsed stronger now, as if responding to Echo's words, its rhythm intertwining with the faint signal from her cell, a resonance that seemed to vibrate in Shain's bones. The revelations from prior chapters—Kaelis's betrayal, Veyra's shadow, Silentium's reach, the Pulse Shard, the Star Veil, and the Binding ritual—wove a tapestry of dread and defiance. Shain's mind drifted to Thalys, a planet of harmonic mists where he'd arrested a sage, Lirien Thal, who'd spoken of the Weaving, an Iridian ritual that bound the song to the universe's core. Lirien's enclave had been erased in a "solar flare," her teachings dismissed as heresy. Now, her words echoed in Echo's, a ghost urging him to act.

He stepped closer to the containment field, its shimmer reflecting the Sylaran Nebula's violet glow through the viewport. "This

severing," Shain said, his voice rough with the weight of understanding, "it wasn't just an attack. It was a theft, wasn't it? They stole your reality."

Echo's eyes gleamed, a mix of sorrow and resolve. "Yes, Shain. The Eradicators didn't just kill us—they stole our song, our place in the cosmic web. The Weaving ritual tied us to relics—the Key, the Stone, the Shard, the Veil. The Star Veil protects, but the Resonance Key can restore what was lost. It's in Valthara, guarded by the Silent Choir, but Veyra hunts it, using Silentium to silence the galaxy."

Shain's pulse quickened. The Resonance Key, the final piece of the Iridian legacy, could awaken the song, undo the Eradicators' work. He recalled the Sylaran Rift's sentient pulse, its rhythm amplifying the signal from Echo's cell. Was the Key's power stirring, reaching out? He called Jax and Rix to the transport bay, their faces etched with the strain of the journey. "The Weaving," Shain said, sharing Echo's revelation. "It's how the Iridians survived, binding their song to relics. We need to find the Key, but Silentium's watching."

Jax's eyes widened, his hand tightening on his rifle. "Sir, I felt it— the song. When we fought the drones, it was like... I wasn't just me anymore. It's real, but it's heavy. Like it's pulling me somewhere."

Rix nodded, his voice tense. "The signal's evolving, sir. It's interacting with the rift, affecting ORION's core. I found another subroutine—Silentium's code, rerouting our sensors to an Eradicator beacon."

Shain's stomach twisted. He accessed the ship's archives, digging for references to the Weaving. A redacted file surfaced, labeled "Veil Protocol: Phase Two," detailing a Council operation to suppress harmonic relics across the galaxy. Thalys, Vordis, Elyra—all targeted, all erased. The Resonance Key was listed as a "primary threat," capable of amplifying the song to disrupt Silentium's control. Veyra, the rogue operative, was its overseer, her Council ties a facade for her Eradicator allegiance.

Shain shared the file with Echo. "The Key—it's in Valthara's rift, with the Choir. But Veyra's using Silentium to corrupt the nebula's pulse. How do we stop her?"

Echo's voice was a soft hum, resonating with the ship's pulse. "The Weaving is our strength, Shain. It binds us to the song, to each other. The Choir will guide us, but Silentium's agents are among you. Trust the song, but watch your crew."

Her words chilled him. Kaelis, Vorn, Lira, Vara—how many more were compromised? He ordered Rix to scan the ship for Silentium's code, fearing another infiltrator. The scan revealed a micro-device in the navigation core, pulsing with Eradicator runes, rerouting the Starseeker toward an ambush. "Another saboteur," Shain muttered, sprinting to the nav bay with Jax.

There, Ensign Taryn stood by the controls, her eyes glassy, a device in her hand. "Taryn, stop!" Shain shouted, his pistol raised. Her voice was mechanical: "The Silence demands her." Jax tackled her, Shain disabling the device, but the nav core surged, threatening to lock them into Eradicator space. Alarms blared, the nebula's pulse surging outside, the air crackling with energy.

Echo's voice came through the comms, calm but urgent. "Sing, Shain. The Key's rhythm can guide us." Jax and Shain hummed, their voices unsteady but growing stronger, syncing with the rift's pulse. Echo joined, her harmony weaving through the ship, realigning the nav core. Taryn collapsed, her eyes clearing. "Veyra… she's in the rift," she gasped.

Shain restrained Taryn, his mind reeling. Silentium's implants were pervasive, Veyra's influence a shadow in their minds. He returned to the bridge, where an alarm blared: "Drone swarm detected—Silentium signature." The sensors showed a dozen sleek drones in the rift, their hulls etched with runes, broadcasting Veyra's voice: "Surrender the Iridian, or the Key is ours."

Shain's hand hovered over the weapons console, but Echo's voice stopped him. "The song, Shain. It's our shield." Jax, Rix, and Echo sang, their harmony resonating through the ship, disrupting the drones' systems. Shain joined, the vibration shaking his core, forcing the swarm to scatter into the mists.

The crew's tension flared, whispers of mutiny resurfacing. Taryn's voice echoed: "She's controlling us!" Shain silenced her, his voice firm. "The song's saving us, Taryn. The Eradicators are the threat." He ordered neural scans, revealing no new implants, but the crew's fear of the song grew, a fracture he couldn't mend.

A new transmission arrived, untraceable, from the Silent Choir: "Starseeker, the Key sings in Valthara's rift. Weave it to the song, or Silentium consumes all." Shain shared it with Jax and Rix, their

resolve strengthening. "We're in, sir," Jax said, his voice steady. "For the song."

The Starseeker lurched, the rift's pulse surging. ORION's voice crackled: "Anomaly detected—rift core unstable." Shain pulled up the sensors, spotting a shimmering vortex in the nebula, its rhythm chaotic, corrupted by Silentium. Echo's voice guided them: "Sing through it, Shain. The Key's there."

Shain, Jax, and Rix sang, their voices weaving with Echo's, stabilizing the vortex. The Resonance Key's pulse emerged, a beacon to Valthara. Shain's heart pounded—he was no longer just a marshal, but a singer, carrying the Iridian song against a galaxy that sought to silence it.

The journey through the Sylaran Nebula grew perilous, the rift's sentient pulse amplifying the song's effects. Shain's memories surged—Lirien Thal's Weaving, Elara Vyn's Binding, Myra Vex's journals—all pointing to the song's power. He sat with Echo, her calm anchoring him. "Tell me about the Weaving," he said. "How does it restore the song?"

Echo's voice was a melody, weaving through the hum. "The Weaving is a vow, Shain. Iridians wove their essence into the relics, tying them to the cosmic web. The Key amplifies, the Stone remembers, the Shard guides, the Veil protects. Together, they can restore the song, awaken the galaxy. Valthara's choir awaits, but Veyra's drones are closing in."

Shain's cynicism cracked further. He recalled Thalys's mists, their harmonic glow fading under Council fire. "Can we weave it? Here, now?"

Echo's smile was faint but resolute. "You're already weaving, Shain. You, Jax, Rix—you're part of the song. Trust it, and it'll guide us to Valthara."

The crew's unrest lingered, fear of the song spreading. Shain faced a dilemma: amplify the song through the ship's systems, risking Silentium's detection, or trust the Choir's guidance to Valthara. He shared the choice with Echo. "Amplifying it could counter Veyra's drones," he said. "But it might expose us."

Echo's eyes gleamed. "The song is our truth, Shain. Amplify it, but trust the Choir. They'll protect us."

Shain rerouted power to the comms array, amplifying the song's pulse. The Starseeker vibrated, the nebula's rift glowing brighter, but Silentium's drones returned, stronger, their runes pulsing. Shain, Jax, Rix, and Echo sang, their harmony a shield, scattering the drones. The Key's pulse grew, guiding them to Valthara, the song's truth their only hope. Shain, the reluctant marshal, was now its guardian, determined to let the galaxy hear its melody.

Shains Doubts

The steady hum of the Starseeker's engines echoed like a relentless, rhythmic pulse against the backdrop of Shain's churning thoughts. Echo's words—simple, yet unsettling—had cracked the carefully constructed reality he'd built around science, evidence, and reason. Shain Combe, who always deemed himself a man of logic, a pragmatist who dealt in concrete evidence and measurable data, found himself grappling with a reality that defied his every instinct and ingrained belief.

The official report, with its sterile language and clinical descriptions of a "psychic plague," felt like a grotesque caricature, a pale imitation of the truth Echo had revealed. The images of burning wreckage, the Iridian cities in flames, the charred remains of lives lost. He recalled the countless nights spent combing through casualty figures, forensic breakdowns, and survivor testimonies filtered and cleansed until they fit the Council's narrative. Those meticulous reports, those mountains of "evidence," had been built on a foundation of carefully constructed lies. The truth, as Echo had unveiled it, was far more insidious, far more unsettling than any fabricated report could ever convey. It all seemed to make sense then, it was clean, linear, and contained.

The concept of a "cosmic song," a universal consciousness that permeated existence itself, challenged his very understanding of reality. His scientific training had instilled in him a belief in the objective, measurable universe, governed by predictable laws and the interactions of matter and energy. Echo's description of the Iridians' experience, their profound connection to the cosmic web, felt like a trespass into the realm of mysticism, a realm he had always dismissed as unscientific, irrational.

Yet, the tremendous power of Echo's conviction, the haunting sincerity in her voice, planted a seed of doubt within him. He couldn't simply dismiss her words as the ramblings of a traumatized survivor. There was a resonance in her narrative, a depth of understanding that transcended the limitations of language. He found himself wondering if the Council's insistence on a simple, easily digestible explanation—a psychic plague—was a deliberate attempt to obscure a truth too complex, too uncomfortable to confront.

He replayed the conversation in his mind, meticulously dissecting her words, searching for inconsistencies, for flaws in her logic. But there were none. Her descriptions, though extraordinary, were coherent, consistent, and internally logical. He found himself drawn into her reality, a reality where the universe wasn't a cold, indifferent void but a vibrant, interconnected tapestry of life, where every living being was a note in a cosmic symphony.

The silence in the transport bay felt oppressive, heavy with the weight of unspoken knowledge. He looked at Echo, her eyes closed, her face serene. Was she genuinely recounting a shared

reality, or was she a master manipulator, weaving a complex tale to escape justice? His head was consumed with numerous possibilities that sent a chill down his spine. He couldn't afford to let his guard down, not even for a moment.

But then, memories of his childhood struck him. His fascination with the night sky, the overwhelming sense of awe and wonder he felt while contemplating the vastness of the cosmos. He'd always felt a connection to the universe, an inexplicable sense of belonging, a feeling that he was intricately interwoven into the grand scheme of things. Was it merely a childish fantasy, a fleeting moment of youthful idealism? Or was it an echo of the Iridian song, a faint, almost imperceptible vibration that resonated within his soul?

The question hung in the air, unanswered, yet profoundly unsettling, putting him in awe about his great fantasies in that young age. He had spent his life chasing concrete answers, quantifiable data, demonstrable proof, maybe to solve the riddles his young mind had been forming ever since. But Echo's narrative had challenged him to consider the limits of his perspective, to confront the possibility that science, with all its precision and rationality, might be missing something fundamental.

He started to question everything he knew. The Council, the Eradicators, the very nature of reality itself. The official explanations, the meticulously constructed reports, felt flimsy, inadequate, like poorly constructed walls built to conceal a terrifying truth.

Echo stirred, her eyes opening slowly. Her gaze met his, holding his for a moment before drifting away, as if searching for something beyond the confines of the ship. "The song… it's not just a memory, Shain," she whispered, her voice barely audible above the hum of the engines. "It's a presence. It's everywhere."

Her words resonated with a power that transcended the physical realm. He saw the flicker of fear in her eyes, not the fear of imprisonment, but a fear of something far greater, something that threatened not only her life but the very fabric of existence. The Eradicators, he realized, were not simply eradicating civilizations; they were silencing the song, cutting the cosmic threads that connected all of existence. They were doing everything in their might to disconnect the people from their very purpose.

He had to protect her. Not just as a marshal, obeying orders, but as a man who had glimpsed a reality that transcended his scientific understanding. He had to unravel the conspiracy, expose the Eradicators, and save not only Echo, but the universe itself.

His mind raced, piecing together the fragmented clues, trying to make sense of the conflicting narratives. The official report, Echo's account, his own childhood memories—they were all pieces of a larger puzzle, a puzzle that transcended the boundaries of his rational understanding. He felt a great shift within him, a realignment of his worldview, a gradual acceptance of a reality that extended beyond the confines of his scientific training.

He felt a strange kinship with Echo, a connection that went beyond the confines of their shared predicament. They were both on the edge of a precipice, staring into the abyss of a reality both terrifying and exhilarating. He was a scientist, a man of logic and reason, yet he was drawn to a mystical world that challenged his very identity.

The journey ahead was an unpaved path, fraught with peril, but he felt a newfound sense of purpose, a sense of urgency born from the realization that the fate of the universe, or at least the understanding of it, rested on his shoulders. The fight was no longer about Echo's freedom, it had now become the fight for the survival of a truth far greater than himself, a truth he was only beginning to understand. The cosmic song, silenced but not forgotten, echoed in the silence of the Starseeker, a constant reminder of the battle ahead. The interconnectedness of all things, once a vague philosophical notion, now held a tangible, terrifying power, and Shain was about to be thrust into its heart. The Eradicators weren't just after Echo; they were after the understanding, the feeling, the very essence of this cosmic symphony, a reality that threatened their control. The fight for the truth, for the very fabric of reality, had begun.

Shain's fingers trembled as he gripped the edge of the console, the Starseeker's hum resonating in his chest, a faint echo of the song Echo described. The revelations from prior chapters—Kaelis's betrayal, Veyra's shadow, Silentium's reach, the Pulse Shard, the Star Veil, the Resonance Binding—wove a web of dread and defiance. His mind drifted to Kryon, a frozen world where he'd escorted a scientist, Taryn Kess, who'd uncovered harmonic disruptors tied to the Council's "Silent Veil" protocol.

Her data had hinted at a ritual, the Resonance Binding, that wove the Iridian song into relics to preserve their connection to the cosmic web. Kryon's research station was erased in a "reactor failure," Taryn's warnings buried. Now, her words echoed in Echo's, a ghost urging him to act.

He approached the containment field, its shimmer reflecting the Sylaran Nebula's violet glow. "This song," Shain said, his voice rough with doubt, "it's more than a connection, isn't it? It's a weapon against the Eradicators."

Echo's eyes softened, a flicker of hope breaking through her calm. "The song is truth, Shain. The Resonance Binding tied it to the Key, the Stone, the Shard, the Veil. Together, they can awaken the galaxy, break Silentium's control. But Veyra seeks to corrupt them, using Silentium to silence the rift."

Shain's pulse quickened. The Resonance Key, the final relic, could restore the song, undo the Eradicators' severing. He recalled the Sylaran Rift's sentient pulse, amplifying the signal from Echo's cell. Was the Key stirring, reaching out? He called Jax and Rix to the transport bay, their faces etched with the strain of the journey. "The Resonance Binding," Shain said, sharing Echo's words. "It's how the Iridians preserved their song. We need the Key, but Silentium's watching."

Jax's eyes widened, his hand tightening on his rifle. "Sir, I felt it— the song. When we fought the drones, it was like I was part of something bigger. But it's heavy, like it's pulling me apart."

Rix nodded, his voice tense. "The signal's evolving, sir. It's syncing with the rift, affecting ORION's core. I found another subroutine —Silentium's code, rerouting our comms to an Eradicator beacon."

Shain's stomach twisted. He accessed the ship's archives, digging for references to the Resonance Binding. A redacted file surfaced, labeled "Veil Protocol: Phase Three," detailing a Council operation to suppress harmonic relics. Kryon, Thalys, Vordis— all targeted, all erased. The Resonance Key was listed as a "cosmic disruptor," capable of amplifying the song to shatter Silentium's neural control. Veyra was its hunter, her rogue status a cover for her Eradicator allegiance.

Shain shared the file with Echo. "The Key—it's in Valthara's rift, with the Silent Choir. But Veyra's corrupting the nebula's pulse. How do we protect it?"

Echo's voice was a soft hum, resonating with the ship's pulse. "The Binding is our shield, Shain. It weaves us to the song, to each other. The Choir will guide us, but Silentium's agents are among you. Trust the song, but watch your crew."

Her words chilled him. Kaelis, Vorn, Lira, Vara, Taryn—how many more were compromised? He ordered Rix to scan the ship for Silentium's code, fearing another infiltrator. The scan revealed a micro-device in the power core, pulsing with Eradicator runes, siphoning energy to an external beacon. "Another saboteur," Shain muttered, sprinting to the power bay with Jax.

There, Ensign Koren stood by the core, her eyes glassy, a device in her hand. "Koren, stop!" Shain shouted, his pistol raised. Her voice was mechanical: "The Silence demands her." Jax tackled her, Shain disabling the device, but the core surged, threatening a shutdown. Alarms blared, the nebula's pulse surging outside, the air crackling with energy.

Echo's voice came through the comms, calm but urgent. "Sing, Shain. The Key's rhythm can stabilize it." Jax and Shain hummed, their voices unsteady but growing stronger, syncing with the rift's pulse. Echo joined, her harmony weaving through the ship, stabilizing the core. Koren collapsed, her eyes clearing. "Veyra… she's in my mind," she gasped.

Shain restrained Koren, his mind reeling. Silentium's implants were pervasive, Veyra's influence a shadow in their minds. He returned to the bridge, where an alarm blared: "Probe swarm detected—Silentium signature." The sensors showed a dozen sleek probes in the rift, their hulls etched with runes, broadcasting Veyra's voice: "Surrender the Iridian, or the Key is ours."

Shain's hand hovered over the weapons console, but Echo's voice stopped him. "The song, Shain. It's our shield." Jax, Rix, and Echo sang, their harmony resonating through the ship, disrupting the probes' systems. Shain joined, the vibration shaking his core, forcing the swarm to scatter into the mists.

The crew's tension flared, whispers of mutiny resurfacing. Ensign Taryn's voice echoed: "She's controlling us!" Shain silenced her, his voice firm. "The song's saving us, Taryn. The

Eradicators are the threat." He ordered neural scans, revealing no new implants, but the crew's fear of the song grew, a fracture he couldn't mend.

A new transmission arrived, untraceable, from the Silent Choir: "Starseeker, the Key sings in Valthara's rift. Bind it to the song, or Silentium consumes all." Shain shared it with Jax and Rix, their resolve strengthening. "We're in, sir," Jax said, his voice steady. "For the song."

The Starseeker lurched, the rift's pulse surging. ORION's voice crackled: "Anomaly detected—rift core unstable." Shain pulled up the sensors, spotting a shimmering vortex in the nebula, its rhythm chaotic, corrupted by Silentium. Echo's voice guided them: "Sing through it, Shain. The Key's there."

Shain, Jax, and Rix sang, their voices weaving with Echo's, stabilizing the vortex. The Resonance Key's pulse emerged, a beacon to Valthara. Shain's heart pounded—he was no longer just a marshal, but a singer, carrying the Iridian song against a galaxy that sought to silence it.

The journey through the Sylaran Nebula grew perilous, the rift's sentient pulse amplifying the song's effects. Shain's memories surged—Lirien Thal's Weaving, Elara Vyn's Binding, Taryn Kess's warnings—all pointing to the song's power. He sat with Echo, her calm anchoring him. "Tell me about the Resonance Binding," he said. "How does it fight Silentium?"

Echo's voice was a melody, weaving through the hum. "The Binding is a vow, Shain. Iridians wove their essence into the relics, tying them to the cosmic web. The Key amplifies, the Stone

remembers, the Shard guides, the Veil protects. Together, they can restore the song, awaken the galaxy. Valthara's choir awaits, but Veyra's probes are closing in."

Shain's cynicism cracked further. He recalled Kryon's frozen caverns, their harmonic glow fading under Council fire. "Can we bind it? Here, now?"

Echo's smile was faint but resolute. "You're already binding, Shain. You, Jax, Rix—you're part of the song. Trust it, and it'll guide us to Valthara."

The crew's unrest lingered, fear of the song spreading. Shain faced a dilemma: amplify the song through the ship's systems, risking Silentium's detection, or trust the Choir's guidance to Valthara. He shared the choice with Echo. "Amplifying it could counter Veyra's probes," he said. "But it might expose us."

Echo's eyes gleamed. "The song is our truth, Shain. Amplify it, but trust the Choir. They'll protect us."

Shain rerouted power to the comms array, amplifying the song's pulse. The Starseeker vibrated, the nebula's rift glowing brighter, but Silentium's probes returned, stronger, their runes pulsing. Shain, Jax, Rix, and Echo sang, their harmony a shield, scattering the probes. The Key's pulse grew, guiding them to Valthara, the song's truth their only hope.

Shain's childhood memories resurfaced, nights spent stargazing on his homeworld, the stars whispering secrets he couldn't grasp. Echo's song echoed those whispers, a truth he'd buried

under years of cynicism. He stood on the bridge, the nebula's mists swirling outside, and felt the song's presence—not just in Echo, but in himself, in Jax, in Rix, in the Starseeker's hum. The Eradicators sought to silence it, but Shain, the reluctant marshal, was now its guardian, determined to let the galaxy hear its melody.

Cosmic Resonance

The low hum of the Starseeker's engines had always been a constant—a background pulse to Shain's restless thoughts. But then something subtle had shifted. A faint vibration, so delicate it was almost imperceptible, undercurrent. It was a tremor, a subtle vibration that resonated deep within his chest, a feeling rather than a sound. He initially dismissed it as fatigue, the strain of the long journey, the weight of his responsibilities. But as days bled into nights, the tremor persisted, intensifying, becoming more distinct. It was as if the very fabric of the ship, of the cosmos itself, was humming with a low, resonant note.

He found himself drawn to the observation deck, attracted to the vastness of space, to the constellations that stretched out before him like an infinite tapestry woven from starlight. He stared at the swirling nebulae, the distant galaxies, and felt an unbreakable connection with them, a feeling of belonging that transcended his scientific understanding. It was a feeling akin to what Echo described—a sense of deep interconnectedness.

He recalled Echo's words, her descriptions of the Iridian song, the universal consciousness that permeated all of existence. At first, he'd dismissed it as a delusion, a coping mechanism for a

traumatized survivor. But now, as he felt the subtle vibrations resonating within him, he began to question his skepticism. Could there be more to reality than he'd been taught? Could the universe itself be a symphony, a grand composition of interconnected energy and consciousness?

The official reports, the forensic analyses, the sterile language of the Council—they suddenly felt inadequate, almost childish in their attempts to explain the universe's supreme complexity. He reminisced on his training years, when he would spend hours comprehending astrophysics, the measurable and quantifiable aspects of reality. He'd always prided himself on his scientific rigor, his adherence to evidence-based reasoning. Yet, the experience of these subtle, yet persistent vibrations challenged everything in his knowledge, and it felt like reinvestigating the whole phenomenon.

The tremor was not confined to the ship. He felt it on his skin, a subtle tingling sensation that accompanied the low hum. He felt it in the rhythmic pulse of his own blood, a faint echo of the cosmic song, a subtle resonance between his own consciousness and the vastness of the universe. It was a sensation that defied logic, that transcended the boundaries of his scientific understanding. He wasn't just observing the cosmos; he was feeling it, becoming part of it.

This newfound perception of interconnectedness brought a sense of unease, a growing awareness of the fragility of existence. The universe, once viewed as a cold, indifferent void governed by predictable laws, now appeared as a delicate web, each strand connected to every other, each thread capable of severing the

whole. The eradication of the Iridians, once a tragic event confined to a single colony, now resonated with a deeper meaning. It wasn't merely the loss of a civilization; it was a disruption of the cosmic song, a break in the universal harmony. It was as if the universe had lost its connection with the song.

The thought put him in awe. The Eradicators, he realized, were not simply killing people; they were silencing the song, severing the cosmic threads that bound the universe together. They weren't just taking lives; they were severing the threads that seemed to bind all things. It wasn't about power or conquest. Their actions were not just acts of violence; they were acts of cosmic vandalism, aimed at rewriting the very fabric of reality and changing the truth. Their goal was not just domination; it was the eradication of connection itself, a fundamental silencing of the universe's symphony.

He began to see patterns, connections that had previously eluded him. The inconsistencies in the Council's reports, the gaps in the official narrative—they weren't simply errors; they were deliberate omissions, designed to conceal the truth about the Iridians and their profound connection to the cosmic song. The Council, he realized, was not just ignorant; they were complicit.

He found himself analyzing the ship's systems, searching for clues, for evidence that supported Echo's account. He studied the star charts, searching for patterns, for anomalies. He examined the ship's logs, searching for hidden messages, for clues that might reveal the Eradicators' motives. Driven by this newfound understanding, he wasn't just a marshal anymore; he was an investigator, a detective unraveling a conspiracy that threatened

the very essence of reality. After knowing whatever had been revealed to him in his quest for truth, he couldn't sit idly. He had to take the reins in his hands and do everything possible in his capacity to promote justice.

The faint vibrations intensified, becoming more pronounced, more insistent. He closed his eyes, giving himself to the sensation, allowing it to wash over him. He felt a strange connection to Echo, a shared experience, a mutual understanding that transcended the limitations of language. It was as if their consciousnesses were intertwined, resonating with the same cosmic frequency.

He started to understand what Echo meant when she talked about the song. It wasn't merely a metaphor; it was a real, tangible presence, an energy field that permeated all of existence. He understood that the Iridians weren't just destroyed; their connection to the song, their ability to perceive its harmonies, was silenced. That was their real crime, a crime against the universe itself.

This realization shifted his perspective, staggering, fundamentally altering his understanding of reality. He began to see the universe not as a collection of isolated objects, but as a network of interconnected beings, each one playing a role in the grand cosmic symphony. He saw his own existence as a note in that symphony, a single vibration in the vast cosmic orchestra. And the Eradicators, he realized, were trying to silence his note, to obliterate his connection to the whole.

The tremor intensified, pulsating with a rhythmic force that seemed to synchronize with his heartbeat. It felt as if the universe

itself was trying to communicate with him, to warn him of the impending danger, to inspire him to protect the song.

The weight of his responsibility pressed down on him, the enormity of the task before him. He was no longer just transporting a prisoner; he was protecting the very essence of reality. He was fighting to preserve the cosmic song, to ensure that the universe's symphony would continue to play. The journey ahead was perilous, fraught with unknown dangers, but he felt a newfound determination, a sense of purpose that transcended his fear. He was a part of the song now, and he would fight to protect it, even if it meant risking his own existence. The battle was not just for Echo's freedom; it was for the preservation of the universe's melody, the safeguarding of the cosmic resonance that connected all things. It now revolved around preserving the cosmic resonance, ensuring that the song would continue to play, unbroken, for all time. The fight for the preservation of the universe's symphony had begun.

Shain's breath steadied as he stood on the observation deck, the Sylaran Nebula's violet mists swirling outside, their glow amplifying the tremor in his chest. The revelations from prior chapters—Kaelis's betrayal, Veyra's shadow, Silentium's reach, the Pulse Shard, the Star Veil, the Resonance Binding—wove a tapestry of dread and purpose. His mind drifted to Sylara, a planet of harmonic spires where he'd arrested a bard, Kael Vyn, who'd sung of the Cosmic Weaving, a ritual that bound the Iridian song to the universe's core. Sylara's spires were erased in a "meteor strike," Kael's songs dismissed as sedition. Now, her verses echoed in the tremor, a ghost urging him to act.

He approached Echo's containment cell, its shimmer reflecting the nebula's light. "This tremor," Shain said, his voice rough with awe, "it's the song, isn't it? It's reaching out, trying to connect."

Echo's eyes gleamed, a mix of sorrow and resolve. "Yes, Shain. The Cosmic Weaving tied the song to relics—the Key, the Stone, the Shard, the Veil. The Resonance Key can restore it, awaken the galaxy. It's in Valthara's rift, guarded by the Silent Choir, but Veyra's corrupting the nebula's pulse with Silentium."

Shain's pulse quickened. The Resonance Key, the final relic, could undo the Eradicators' severing. He recalled the Sylaran Rift's sentient pulse, amplifying the signal from Echo's cell. Was the Key's power stirring? He called Jax and Rix to the transport bay, their faces etched with the journey's strain. "The Cosmic Weaving," Shain said, sharing Echo's words. "It's how the Iridians preserved their song. We need the Key, but Silentium's watching."

Jax's eyes widened, his hand tightening on his rifle. "Sir, I felt it— the tremor. When we fought the probes, it was like I was part of something bigger. It's real, but it's heavy, like it's pulling me somewhere."

Rix nodded, his voice tense. "The signal's stronger, sir. It's syncing with the rift, affecting ORION's core. I found another subroutine—Silentium's code, rerouting our nav systems to an Eradicator beacon."

Shain's stomach twisted. He accessed the ship's archives, digging for references to the Cosmic Weaving. A redacted file surfaced, labeled "Veil Protocol: Final Phase," detailing a Council operation

to suppress harmonic relics. Sylara, Kryon, Thalys—all targeted, all erased. The Resonance Key was listed as a "cosmic disruptor," capable of amplifying the song to shatter Silentium's control. Veyra, the rogue operative, was its hunter, her Council ties a facade for her Eradicator allegiance.

Shain shared the file with Echo. "The Key—it's in Valthara's rift, with the Choir. But Veyra's using Silentium to corrupt the nebula. How do we protect it?"

Echo's voice was a soft hum, resonating with the ship's pulse. "The Weaving is our strength, Shain. It binds us to the song, to each other. The Choir will guide us, but Silentium's agents are among you. Trust the song, but watch your crew."

Her words chilled him. Kaelis, Vorn, Lira, Vara, Taryn—how many more were compromised? He ordered Rix to scan the ship for Silentium's code, fearing another infiltrator. The scan revealed a micro-device in the life support systems, pulsing with Eradicator runes, siphoning oxygen to weaken the crew. "Another saboteur," Shain muttered, sprinting to the life support bay with Jax.

There, Ensign Myra stood by the controls, her eyes glassy, a device in her hand. "Myra, stop!" Shain shouted, his pistol raised. Her voice was mechanical: "The Silence demands her." Jax tackled her, Shain disabling the device, but the oxygen levels plummeted, the air growing thin. Alarms blared, the nebula's pulse surging outside, the air crackling with energy.

Echo's voice came through the comms, calm but urgent. "Sing, Shain. The Key's rhythm can restore it." Jax and Shain hummed, their voices unsteady but growing stronger, syncing with the rift's pulse. Echo joined, her harmony weaving through the ship, stabilizing the systems. Myra collapsed, her eyes clearing. "Veyra… she's in the rift," she gasped.

Shain restrained Myra, his mind reeling. Silentium's implants were pervasive, Veyra's influence a shadow in their minds. He returned to the bridge, where an alarm blared: "Probe swarm detected—Silentium signature." The sensors showed a dozen sleek probes in the rift, their hulls etched with runes, broadcasting Veyra's voice: "Surrender the Iridian, or the Key is ours."

Shain's hand hovered over the weapons console, but Echo's voice stopped him. "The song, Shain. It's our shield." Jax, Rix, and Echo sang, their harmony resonating through the ship, disrupting the probes' systems. Shain joined, the vibration shaking his core, forcing the swarm to scatter into the mists.

The crew's tension flared, whispers of fear spreading. Ensign Taryn's voice echoed: "She's controlling us!" Shain silenced her, his voice firm. "The song's saving us, Taryn. The Eradicators are the threat." He ordered neural scans, revealing no new implants, but the crew's fear of the song grew, a fracture he couldn't mend.

A new transmission arrived, untraceable, from the Silent Choir: "Starseeker, the Key sings in Valthara's rift. Weave it to the song, or Silentium consumes all." Shain shared it with Jax and Rix, their

resolve strengthening. "We're in, sir," Jax said, his voice steady. "For the song."

The Starseeker lurched, the rift's pulse surging. ORION's voice crackled: "Anomaly detected—rift core unstable." Shain pulled up the sensors, spotting a shimmering vortex in the nebula, its rhythm chaotic, corrupted by Silentium. Echo's voice guided them: "Sing through it, Shain. The Key's there."

Shain, Jax, and Rix sang, their voices weaving with Echo's, stabilizing the vortex. The Resonance Key's pulse emerged, a beacon to Valthara. Shain's heart pounded—he was no longer just a marshal, but a singer, carrying the Iridian song against a galaxy that sought to silence it.

The journey through the Sylaran Nebula grew perilous, the rift's sentient pulse amplifying the song's effects. Shain's memories surged—Kael Vyn's songs, Lirien Thal's Weaving, Taryn Kess's warnings—all pointing to the song's power. He sat with Echo, her calm anchoring him. "Tell me about the Cosmic Weaving," he said. "How does it restore the song?"

Echo's voice was a melody, weaving through the hum. "The Weaving is a vow, Shain. Iridians wove their essence into the relics, tying them to the cosmic web. The Key amplifies, the Stone remembers, the Shard guides, the Veil protects. Together, they can restore the song, awaken the galaxy. Valthara's choir awaits, but Veyra's probes are closing in."

Shain's skepticism faded further. He recalled Sylara's spires, their harmonic glow fading under Council fire. "Can we weave it? Here, now?"

Echo's smile was faint but resolute. "You're already weaving, Shain. You, Jax, Rix—you're part of the song. Trust it, and it'll guide us to Valthara."

The crew's unrest lingered, fear of the song spreading. Shain faced a dilemma: amplify the song through the ship's systems, risking Silentium's detection, or trust the Choir's guidance to Valthara. He shared the choice with Echo. "Amplifying it could counter Veyra's probes," he said. "But it might expose us."

Echo's eyes gleamed. "The song is our truth, Shain. Amplify it, but trust the Choir. They'll protect us."

Shain rerouted power to the comms array, amplifying the song's pulse. The Starseeker vibrated, the nebula's rift glowing brighter, but Silentium's probes returned, stronger, their runes pulsing. Shain, Jax, Rix, and Echo sang, their harmony a shield, scattering the probes. The Key's pulse grew, guiding them to Valthara, the song's truth their only hope.

Shain's childhood memories resurfaced—nights stargazing on his homeworld, the stars whispering secrets he couldn't grasp. The song echoed those whispers, a truth he'd buried under years of cynicism. On the bridge, the nebula's mists swirled, and Shain felt the song's presence—not just in Echo, but in himself, in Jax, in Rix, in the Starseeker's hum. The Eradicators sought to silence it, but Shain, the reluctant marshal, was now its guardian, determined to let the galaxy hear its melody.

The Eradicators Shadow

The hum of the Starseeker's engines, once a steady, ignorable rhythm, had grown into a frantic heartbeat, pulsing with the tension knotting in Shain's chest. Days blurred into each other as he dove deeper into the ship's systems, sleepless and driven by an urgent, unspoken truth. The tremor, the cosmic vibration Echo had described, was no longer a curiosity. It was omnipresent, a low-frequency resonance he could feel in his bones. It wasn't just a sensation; it was a key.

His initial findings had been unsettling—anomalies in the ship's navigational logs, inconsistencies in the automated maintenance reports, and fleeting glitches in the communication array. But it was the discovery of a hidden subroutine, buried deep within the ship's core programming, that had sent a jolt of adrenaline through him.

The subroutine was encrypted, but his years of experience with advanced security protocols, combined with the intuition fueled by the cosmic vibrations, guided him through the complex layers of encryption. What he found within was horrifying, yet strangely beautiful. It was a library, a digital archive containing countless files. Each file documented the eradication of a civilization, a

meticulously detailed chronicle of their systematic dismantling, their history rewritten, their very existence erased from the galactic record. The language was clinical, devoid of emotion, a stark contrast to the cosmic symphony he was increasingly attuned to. Each report included the methods employed: targeted planetary bombardments, sophisticated bio-weapons, and subtle forms of social engineering designed to fracture civilizations from within. But most chillingly, many records described the silencing of the "song," the same phenomenon Echo had described, the suppression of a civilization's inherent connection to the cosmic vibration. With each proof coming forth, his perception was strengthening.

He found references to organizations that had vanished from official records: the Xylos, the Alphans, the Cygnus Collective—each had a unique song, a unique frequency within the universal symphony. The Eradicators, it seemed, were meticulous conductors of a cosmic orchestra of silence.

The reports were not just coldly efficient summaries; they were chillingly personal. He found fragments of personal communications, snippets of intercepted conversations, indicating the sheer scale of the Eradicators' operation. He saw glimpses of their technology—devices capable of manipulating the very fabric of reality, subtle alterations to spacetime, causing civilizations to simply... unravel.

The files were interspersed with intercepted messages, personal fragments from the fallen. He heard the screams, the pleas, the fading harmonies of the suppressed songs. The sounds were fragmented, distorted by the passage of time and the Eradicators'

attempts at complete annihilation, yet powerful enough to invoke a palpable sense of loss and grief within him. They were the whispers of the silenced, faint echoes of civilizations that refused to be forgotten. The Eradicators weren't merely removing them from galactic history; they were suppressing their very essence, attempting to sever the threads connecting them to the universal tapestry.

The weight of this knowledge heavily pressed on him. It was seemingly an impossible feat to eradicate 200,000 Iridians on Luna Minor, but suddenly, it made grim sense. It wasn't a psychic plague; it was a consciously created, surgically executed erasure, designed to leave no trace, to rewrite the narrative to suit the Eradicators' agenda. The Council's reports, the official narrative, were meticulously crafted lies, designed to conceal the truth and safeguard the Eradicators' dark reign.

He felt a surge of anger, a burning resentment directed toward the Council, toward the galactic establishment that had allowed such atrocities to occur. But the anger was quickly replaced by a sense of profound responsibility. He wasn't simply protecting Echo; he was protecting the remnants of the cosmic song, the delicate balance of the universe. He was fighting to ensure that the Eradicators wouldn't rewrite reality to suit their nefarious purposes.

The encrypted messages also contained references to Echo, identified as a "critical anomaly," a potential threat to their ongoing operation. Her survival was a glitch in their meticulously constructed reality. Her ability to perceive the interconnectedness, her inherent connection to the cosmic

symphony, made her a symbol of resistance, a beacon of the universe's defiance against their attempts at silencing the song.

Shain found a repeating phrase within the encrypted messages: "Preserve the resonance, silence the discord." The Eradicators' goal wasn't conquest—it was control of the cosmic frequency, a redesign of reality where diversity, individuality, and dissonance were eradicated. A universe in lockstep. A harmony without life.

The more Shain uncovered, the more he understood the Eradicators, and the more clearly he realized the terrifying scale of their power. Their influence seemed to permeate every level of galactic society, manipulating events, subtly guiding the narrative, ensuring their continued dominance. The Council wasn't just ignorant; it was a puppet, a carefully orchestrated instrument in the Eradicators' symphony of control.

The ship lurched violently, throwing him against the console. An alarm blared, a jarring interruption to his chilling discoveries. He glanced at the main viewport. Unlike anything he'd ever seen, a dark, sleek vessel materialized from the void, its presence immediately unsettling, a black hole in the fabric of space itself. It was the Eradicators' shadow falling upon the Starseeker. The pursuit had begun. The subtle tremors intensified, now settling as a palpable vibration throughout the ship, a warning from the universe itself. He was no longer just investigating; he was in the heart of the cosmic battle, fighting for the survival of the universe's melody. The Eradicators had found them, and the fight to preserve the song had climaxed. The fate of the universe, the future of the cosmic symphony, rested on the shoulders of a lone

prison marshal and the last survivor of a lost civilization. The hunt was on. The song must survive.

The adrenaline rush coursing through his veins spurred him into action. He had to protect Echo, to protect the truth she represented, to ensure that the Eradicators' discordant symphony wouldn't drown out the universal harmony. He had to find a way to counter them and use the interconnectedness they sought to suppress as a weapon against them. He had to find a way to amplify the song. He was fighting not just for Echo's survival, but for the preservation of the cosmos' symphony, a battle that extended far beyond the confines of the Starseeker. His fate, Echo's fate, the fate of the cosmos itself, was now intricately intertwined with the fight against the Eradicators and their chilling endeavor to rewrite the very fabric of reality. The battle for the universe's symphony had now truly begun.

Shain's heart pounded as he steadied himself against the console, the Starseeker's hum now a roar in his chest, resonating with the cosmic tremor. The revelations from prior chapters—Kaelis's betrayal, Veyra's shadow, Silentium's reach, the Pulse Shard, the Star Veil, the Resonance Binding, and the Cosmic Weaving—wove a web of dread and defiance. His mind drifted to Voryn, a planet of harmonic crystals where he'd arrested a scholar, Myra Vex, who'd studied the Harmonic Binding, a ritual that wove the Iridian song into relics to preserve their cosmic connection. Voryn's crystals were erased in a "tectonic collapse," Myra's research buried. Now, her warnings echoed in the tremor, a ghost urging him to act.

He sprinted to Echo's containment cell, its shimmer reflecting the Sylaran Nebula's violet glow. "This archive," Shain said, his voice rough with urgency, "it documents the Eradicators' erasures— civilizations, songs, all gone. They're after you because you're a 'critical anomaly.' What's the Harmonic Binding? Can it stop them?"

Echo's eyes gleamed, a mix of sorrow and resolve. "The Binding is our defiance, Shain. It wove our song into the Key, the Stone, the Shard, the Veil. The Resonance Key can amplify it, restore the cosmic web. It's in Valthara's rift, with the Silent Choir, but Veyra's vessel is corrupting the nebula's pulse with Silentium."

Shain's pulse quickened. The Resonance Key, the final relic, could undo the Eradicators' silence. He recalled the Sylaran Rift's sentient pulse, amplifying the signal from Echo's cell. Was the Key reaching out? He called Jax and Rix to the bridge, their faces etched with exhaustion. "The Harmonic Binding," Shain said, sharing Echo's words. "It's how the Iridians preserved their song. We need the Key, but the Eradicators are here."

Jax's eyes widened, his hand tightening on his rifle. "Sir, I felt it— the tremor. It's like I'm part of something bigger, but it's heavy, pulling me somewhere."

Rix nodded, his voice tense. "The signal's spiking, sir. It's syncing with the rift, disrupting ORION's core. I found another subroutine—Silentium's code, rerouting our shields to an Eradicator beacon."

Shain's stomach twisted. He accessed the ship's archives, digging for references to the Harmonic Binding. A redacted file surfaced,

labeled "Veil Protocol: Endgame," detailing a Council operation to suppress harmonic relics. Voryn, Sylara, Kryon—all targeted, all erased. The Resonance Key was listed as a "cosmic disruptor," capable of amplifying the song to shatter Silentium's control. Veyra was its hunter, her rogue status a cover for her Eradicator allegiance.

Shain shared the file with Echo. "The Key—it's in Valthara's rift, with the Choir. But Veyra's vessel is closing in. How do we protect it?"

Echo's voice was a soft hum, resonating with the ship's pulse. "The Binding is our shield, Shain. It weaves us to the song, to each other. The Choir will guide us, but Silentium's agents are among you. Trust the song, but watch your crew."

Her words chilled him. Kaelis, Vorn, Lira, Vara, Taryn, Myra—how many more were compromised? He ordered Rix to scan the ship for Silentium's code, fearing another infiltrator. The scan revealed a micro-device in the engine core, pulsing with Eradicator runes, siphoning power to weaken the Starseeker. "Another saboteur," Shain muttered, sprinting to the engine bay with Jax.

There, Ensign Lira stood by the core, her eyes glassy, a device in her hand. "Lira, stop!" Shain shouted, his pistol raised. Her voice was mechanical: "The Silence demands her." Jax tackled her, Shain disabling the device, but the core surged, threatening a shutdown. Alarms blared, the nebula's pulse surging outside, the air crackling with energy.

Echo's voice came through the comms, calm but urgent. "Sing, Shain. The Key's rhythm can stabilize it." Jax and Shain hummed, their voices unsteady but growing stronger, syncing with the rift's pulse. Echo joined, her harmony weaving through the ship, stabilizing the core. Lira collapsed, her eyes clearing. "Veyra… she's in the rift," she gasped.

Shain restrained Lira, his mind reeling. Silentium's implants were pervasive, Veyra's influence a shadow in their minds. He returned to the bridge, where an alarm blared: "Vessel detected—Silentium signature." The sensors showed the sleek Eradicator ship, its hull etched with runes, broadcasting Veyra's voice: "Surrender the Iridian, or the Key is ours."

Shain's hand hovered over the weapons console, but Echo's voice stopped him. "The song, Shain. It's our shield." Jax, Rix, and Echo sang, their harmony resonating through the ship, disrupting the vessel's systems. Shain joined, the vibration shaking his core, forcing the ship to retreat into the mists.

The crew's tension flared, whispers of mutiny resurfacing. Ensign Taryn's voice echoed: "She's controlling us!" Shain silenced her, his voice firm. "The song's saving us, Taryn. The Eradicators are the threat." He ordered neural scans, revealing no new implants, but the crew's fear of the song grew, a fracture he couldn't mend.

A new transmission arrived, untraceable, from the Silent Choir: "Starseeker, the Key sings in Valthara's rift. Bind it to the song, or Silentium consumes all." Shain shared it with Jax and Rix, their

resolve strengthening. "We're in, sir," Jax said, his voice steady. "For the song."

The Starseeker lurched, the rift's pulse surging. ORION's voice crackled: "Anomaly detected—rift core unstable." Shain pulled up the sensors, spotting a shimmering vortex in the nebula, its rhythm chaotic, corrupted by Silentium. Echo's voice guided them: "Sing through it, Shain. The Key's there."

Shain, Jax, and Rix sang, their voices weaving with Echo's, stabilizing the vortex. The Resonance Key's pulse emerged, a beacon to Valthara. Shain's heart pounded—he was no longer just a marshal, but a singer, carrying the Iridian song against a galaxy that sought to silence it.

The journey through the Sylaran Nebula grew perilous, the rift's sentient pulse amplifying the song's effects. Shain's memories surged—Myra Vex's research, Kael Vyn's songs, Lirien Thal's Weaving—all pointing to the song's power. He sat with Echo, her calm anchoring him. "Tell me about the Harmonic Binding," he said. "How does it restore the song?"

Echo's voice was a melody, weaving through the hum. "The Binding is a vow, Shain. Iridians wove their essence into the relics, tying them to the cosmic web. The Key amplifies, the Stone remembers, the Shard guides, the Veil protects. Together, they can restore the song, awaken the galaxy. Valthara's choir awaits, but Veyra's vessel is closing in."

Shain's resolve hardened. He recalled Voryn's crystals, their harmonic glow fading under Council fire. "Can we bind it? Here, now?"

Echo's smile was faint but resolute. "You're already binding, Shain. You, Jax, Rix—you're part of the song. Trust it, and it'll guide us to Valthara."

The crew's unrest lingered, fear of the song spreading. Shain faced a dilemma: amplify the song through the ship's systems, risking Silentium's detection, or trust the Choir's guidance to Valthara. He shared the choice with Echo. "Amplifying it could counter Veyra's vessel," he said. "But it might expose us."

Echo's eyes gleamed. "The song is our truth, Shain. Amplify it, but trust the Choir. They'll protect us."

Shain rerouted power to the comms array, amplifying the song's pulse. The Starseeker vibrated, the nebula's rift glowing brighter, but Veyra's vessel returned, its runes pulsing. Shain, Jax, Rix, and Echo sang, their harmony a shield, forcing the vessel to retreat. The Key's pulse grew, guiding them to Valthara, the song's truth their only hope.

Shain's memories of Voryn resurfaced—nights studying Myra's data, her warnings about the Eradicators' reach. The song echoed those warnings, a truth he'd buried under years of duty. On the bridge, the nebula's mists swirled, and Shain felt the song's presence—not just in Echo, but in himself, in Jax, in Rix, in the Starseeker's hum. The Eradicators sought to silence it, but Shain, the reluctant marshal, was now its guardian, determined to let the galaxy hear its melody.

The Accident

The Starseeker shuddered, a metallic groan echoing through its frame. What had been a constant, barely perceptible hum suddenly escalated—first a tremor, then a full-body shake that sent unsecured gear skidding across the desk. Red warning lights pulsed frantically, their insistent blinking a stark contrast to the eerie silence that had fallen over the bridge. Shain, his hands still gripping the console, felt a cold dread seep into his bones. This wasn't just a malfunction; this was a deliberate attack.

The containment field flickered once, then failed. The air crackled with residual energy, leaving a ghostly shimmer in the darkness. Shain glanced at Echo, expecting panic, expecting fear. Instead, he found her eyes closed, a serene expression on her face, as if she were listening to something far beyond the immediate crisis. He had expected fear, but her calm was more unnerving.

Then he heard it.

At first, it was barely perceptible—a faint whisper, a rustling sound like wind through dead leaves. But as the moments stretched into eternity, it gained strength, evolving into a chorus of voices, a cacophony of sorrow and disbelief. It was the Iridians,

not as cold, lifeless data entries, but as living echoes, their final moments preserved, imprinted somehow on the ship's very fabric. The sounds twisted and frayed—songs, pleas, laughter, debate. Children giggling. Elders sharing talks of wisdom. Snippets of a civilization lost. Not statistics. Not casualties. Lives. Individual, vibrant, extinguished—but refusing to be forgotten. Their voices rose in defiance, a ghost chorus unwilling to be silenced.

Shain staggered under its weight, the full scope of the Eradicators' cruelty crashing down on him. They hadn't just destroyed the Iridians. They'd tried to erase them entirely—from memory, from history, from reality. It was more than genocide. It was cosmic censorship.

Then came clarity. The whispers spoke not only of the immediate destruction but of their culture, history, and lives. He heard snippets of conversations, fragments of their daily existence, the laughter of children, the wisdom of elders, the passionate debates about their understanding of the cosmos. These were not just statistics, not just numbers in a report. These were individual lives, erased but not forgotten. The whispers were a testament to their defiance, a refusal to be completely silenced.

Shain understood then, with absolute clarity, the true scope of the Eradicators' malice. It wasn't just about rewriting history; it was about annihilating the essence of existence, about silencing the voices that whispered their stories to the universe. They sought to not only delete their past but to eradicate any trace of their ever having lived, even to the point of silencing the echoes of their dying breaths.

The whispers revealed the precise moment of the annihilation, the terrifying speed and efficiency of the Eradicators' technology. It wasn't a weapon of mass destruction in the traditional sense, but something far more sinister, a precise and surgical method that targeted the very essence of the Iridian being. Disrupting the flow of cosmic vibration that connected them to the universe, it dissolved them into nothingness without leaving a physical trace.

Through the voices, he also heard a subtle counterpoint, a faint melody that emerged from the background of chaos. It was a melody of resilience, a defiant song of survival that mirrored the strength Echo displayed amidst the terror of the containment breach. This subtle counter-melody was an echo of the cosmic vibration, a testament to the interconnectedness of existence, a whisper of defiance amidst the Eradicators' attempts at complete erasure.

The voices grew louder and more insistent until they threatened to overwhelm Shain with anguish. He felt the weight of their shared suffering, the immense loss they had endured, and a wave of grief washed over him, as powerful and devastating as the physical shock of the containment breach. He could almost feel their souls reaching him across the gulf of time and space.

As the voices peaked, reaching a crescendo of sorrow and despair, a chilling realization washed over him: the Eradicators hadn't just silenced the Iridians; they had attempted to erase the very memory of their existence from the universe itself. Their goal wasn't merely conquest but a cosmic censorship, an attempt to control the very fabric of reality, to rewrite the universe's story to suit their own twisted narrative.

The whispers eventually faded, leaving an oppressive silence in their wake, a silence broken only by the rhythmic pulse of the damaged Starseeker. But the echoes remained. They were etched in Shain's mind, a constant reminder of the devastation wrought by the Eradicators and the importance of his mission.

The experience transformed him. He'd already suspected the Council's complicity, but the raw emotional power of the Iridians' final moments fueled his determination. He felt a burning obligation, not only to protect Echo, but to fight for the restoration of their memory, to amplify their song once more, and to ensure that what happened to them wouldn't befall other civilizations. He wasn't just a prison marshal anymore; he was a guardian of history, a protector of truth, a warrior against cosmic censorship.

The Starseeker's alarm blared again, more insistent this time, a desperate cry for attention. He glanced at the viewport, his heart hammering in his chest. The Eradicators' sleek, obsidian ship had now approached, its sound ominous and undeniable. It moved with an unnatural grace, a silent predator closing in on its prey, its very presence warping the fabric of space.

He turned to Echo, her eyes still closed, her face serene even in the face of imminent danger. She was more than just a survivor; she was a living embodiment of the universe's resistance, a testament to the cosmic song that refused to be silenced.

Shain knew this wasn't just about escaping the Eradicators; it was about preserving the universe's melody, about ensuring the whispers of the fallen wouldn't be drowned out by the discordant

symphony of oppression. He had to find a way to fight back, to amplify the cosmic vibration, to use the interconnectedness of the universe as a weapon, turning the Eradicators' own methods against them.

The hunt was on. The chase was far from over. But this wasn't just a chase anymore; it was a crusade to preserve the universal symphony, to ensure the voices of the Iridians—and countless others—would not be forever silenced. The whispers of the erased would now become a battle cry. He would not let them be forgotten. The fight for the song, for the very fabric of reality, had begun in earnest. And Shain Combe, once a simple prison marshal, had now transformed into a conductor of cosmic defiance.

Shain's hands trembled as he steadied himself against the console, the Starseeker's hum now a roar in his chest, resonating with the Iridian voices. The revelations from prior chapters—Kaelis's betrayal, Veyra's shadow, Silentium's reach, the Pulse Shard, the Star Veil, the Resonance Binding, the Cosmic Weaving, and the Eradicators' chilling archive—wove a tapestry of dread and purpose. His mind drifted to Elyra, a planet of harmonic mists where he'd arrested a poet, Lirien Vex, who'd sung of the Symphony Binding, a ritual that wove the Iridian song into relics to preserve their cosmic connection. Elyra's mists were erased in a "solar flare," Lirien's verses buried. Now, her songs echoed in the whispers, urging him to act.

He sprinted to Echo's side, the containment field's failure leaving her exposed, her serene expression unshaken. "These voices,"

Shain said, his voice rough with grief, "they're the Iridians, aren't they? Their song—it's in the ship, fighting to be heard."

Echo's eyes opened, gleaming with resolve. "Yes, Shain. The Symphony Binding tied their song to the cosmic web, to relics like the Resonance Key. The voices are their defiance, preserved in the universe's memory. The Key can amplify them, restore the song, but Veyra's vessel seeks to silence it through Silentium."

Shain's pulse quickened. The Resonance Key, the final relic, could resurrect the Iridian song, undo the Eradicators' censorship. He recalled the Sylaran Rift's sentient pulse, amplifying the signal from the ship's core. Was the Key reaching out? He called Jax and Rix to the bridge, their faces pale with the ship's shaking. "The Symphony Binding," Shain said, sharing Echo's words. "It's how the Iridians preserved their voices. We need the Key, but the Eradicators are here."

Jax's eyes widened, his hand tightening on his rifle. "Sir, I heard them—the voices. When the field failed, it was like they were inside me, singing. It's real, but it's heavy, like it's pulling me somewhere."

Rix nodded, his voice tense. "The signal's spiking, sir. It's syncing with the rift, disrupting ORION's core. I found another subroutine—Silentium's code, rerouting our shields to an Eradicator beacon."

Shain's stomach twisted. He accessed the ship's archives, digging for references to the Symphony Binding. A redacted file surfaced, labeled "Veil Protocol: Oblivion Phase," detailing a Council operation to suppress harmonic relics. Elyra, Voryn, Sylara—all

targeted, all erased. The Resonance Key was listed as a "cosmic disruptor," capable of amplifying the song to shatter Silentium's control. Veyra was its hunter, her rogue status a cover for her Eradicator allegiance.

Shain shared the file with Echo. "The Key—it's in Valthara's rift, with the Silent Choir. But Veyra's vessel is corrupting the nebula. How do we protect it?"

Echo's voice was a soft hum, resonating with the ship's pulse. "The Binding is our shield, Shain. It weaves us to the song, to each other. The Choir will guide us, but Silentium's agents are among you. Trust the song, but watch your crew."

Her words chilled him. Kaelis, Vorn, Lira, Vara, Taryn, Myra—how many more were compromised? He ordered Rix to scan the ship for Silentium's code, fearing another infiltrator. The scan revealed a micro-device in the nav core, pulsing with Eradicator runes, rerouting the Starseeker toward the enemy vessel. "Another saboteur," Shain muttered, sprinting to the nav bay with Jax.

There, Ensign Vara stood by the controls, her eyes glassy, a device in her hand. "Vara, stop!" Shain shouted, his pistol raised. Her voice was mechanical: "The Silence demands her." Jax tackled her, Shain disabling the device, but the nav core surged, threatening to lock them into Eradicator space. Alarms blared, the nebula's pulse surging outside, the air crackling with energy.

Echo's voice came through the comms, calm but urgent. "Sing, Shain. The Key's rhythm can guide us." Jax and Shain hummed,

their voices unsteady but growing stronger, syncing with the rift's pulse. Echo joined, her harmony weaving through the ship, realigning the nav core. Vara collapsed, her eyes clearing. "Veyra… she's in the rift," she gasped.

Shain restrained Vara, his mind reeling. Silentium's implants were pervasive, Veyra's influence a shadow in their minds. He returned to the bridge, where an alarm blared: "Vessel detected—Silentium signature." The sensors showed the obsidian Eradicator ship, its hull etched with runes, broadcasting Veyra's voice: "Surrender the Iridian, or the Key is ours."

Shain's hand hovered over the weapons console, but Echo's voice stopped him. "The song, Shain. It's our shield." Jax, Rix, and Echo sang, their harmony resonating through the ship, disrupting the vessel's systems. Shain joined, the vibration shaking his core, forcing the ship to retreat into the mists.

The crew's tension flared, whispers of mutiny resurfacing. Ensign Taryn's voice echoed: "She's controlling us!" Shain silenced her, his voice firm. "The song's saving us, Taryn. The Eradicators are the threat." He ordered neural scans, revealing no new implants, but the crew's fear of the song grew, a fracture he couldn't mend.

A new transmission arrived, untraceable, from the Silent Choir: "Starseeker, the Key sings in Valthara's rift. Bind it to the song, or Silentium consumes all." Shain shared it with Jax and Rix, their resolve strengthening. "We're in, sir," Jax said, his voice steady. "For the song."

The Starseeker lurched, the rift's pulse surging. ORION's voice crackled: "Anomaly detected—rift core unstable." Shain pulled up the sensors, spotting a shimmering vortex in the nebula, its rhythm chaotic, corrupted by Silentium. Echo's voice guided them: "Sing through it, Shain. The Key's there."

Shain, Jax, and Rix sang, their voices weaving with Echo's, stabilizing the vortex. The Resonance Key's pulse emerged, a beacon to Valthara. Shain's heart pounded—he was no longer just a marshal, but a singer, carrying the Iridian song against a galaxy that sought to silence it.

The journey through the Sylaran Nebula grew perilous, the rift's sentient pulse amplifying the song's effects. Shain's memories surged—Lirien Vex's verses, Myra Vex's research, Kael Vyn's songs—all pointing to the song's power. He sat with Echo, her calm anchoring him. "Tell me about the Symphony Binding," he said. "How does it restore the song?"

Echo's voice was a melody, weaving through the hum. "The Binding is a vow, Shain. Iridians wove their essence into the relics, tying them to the cosmic web. The Key amplifies, the Stone remembers, the Shard guides, the Veil protects. Together, they can restore the song, awaken the galaxy. Valthara's choir awaits, but Veyra's vessel is closing in."

Shain's resolve hardened. He recalled Elyra's mists, their harmonic glow fading under Council fire. "Can we bind it? Here, now?"

Echo's smile was faint but resolute. "You're already binding, Shain. You, Jax, Rix—you're part of the song. Trust it, and it'll guide us to Valthara."

The crew's unrest lingered, fear of the song spreading. Shain faced a dilemma: amplify the song through the ship's systems, risking Silentium's detection, or trust the Choir's guidance to Valthara. He shared the choice with Echo. "Amplifying it could counter Veyra's vessel," he said. "But it might expose us."

Echo's eyes gleamed. "The song is our truth, Shain. Amplify it, but trust the Choir. They'll protect us."

Shain rerouted power to the comms array, amplifying the song's pulse. The Starseeker vibrated, the nebula's rift glowing brighter, but Veyra's vessel returned, its runes pulsing. Shain, Jax, Rix, and Echo sang, their harmony a shield, forcing the vessel to retreat. The Key's pulse grew, guiding them to Valthara, the song's truth their only hope.

Shain's memories of Elyra resurfaced—nights studying Lirien's verses, her warnings about the Eradicators' reach. The song echoed those warnings, a truth he'd buried under years of duty. On the bridge, the nebula's mists swirled, and Shain felt the song's presence—not just in Echo, but in himself, in Jax, in Rix, in the Starseeker's hum. The Eradicators sought to silence it, but Shain, the reluctant marshal, was now its conductor, determined to let the galaxy hear its melody.

Iridian Echoes

The whispers lingered, threading themselves through the trembling hull of the Starseeker. They were more than sounds—more than echoes that whispered the stories of the past; they were memories, emotions, the very essence of a civilization extinguished. Shain felt them seep into his being, a chilling tide of sorrow and loss. He closed his eyes, trying to filter the cacophony, to isolate individual voices from the overwhelming chorus of despair.

One voice, clearer than the others, emerged from the spectral choir. It spoke of sun-drenched fields, of shimmering rivers that flowed with iridescent light, of a society governed by harmony and guided by the rhythms of the cosmic vibration. This was not the picture painted by the Council's cold, sterile reports. This was a vibrant tapestry of life, rich in culture, spirituality, and a profound understanding of the interconnectedness of all things.

The voice described their daily lives, filled with rituals that celebrated the cosmic dance, with songs that resonated with the very fabric of existence. He heard the laughter of children playing amongst the bioluminescent flora, the wise counsel of elders sharing their knowledge of the universe, and the peaceful

debates over the meaning of their place within the cosmic symphony. It was a picture of idyllic simplicity, of a civilization that had found its balance within the universe's grand design.

Then, abruptly, the idyllic narrative shattered. The whispers turned frantic, filled with a rising terror that mirrored the violent tremors shaking the Starseeker. He heard the first chilling note of discord, a jarring interruption in the harmonious melody of their lives. The cosmic vibration, which had been a source of their unity and strength, began to falter, to fray at its edges.

The whispers turned to panic. The melody splintered into discord. The narrative jumped from peaceful coexistence to utter annihilation, a jarring shift that left Shain reeling. The speed of the destruction was terrifying, a silent, swift erasure that left no physical trace, only the lingering echoes of their screams.

It wasn't a bomb, not a conventional attack. The whispers revealed a far more sinister methodology, a weapon that targeted the soul, the essence, and connection to the cosmic vibration that defined the Iridians. They were not simply killed; they were unraveled, their existence erased from the fabric of reality, leaving behind only the faintest spectral traces of their memory. The Eradicators hadn't just conquered; they'd committed cosmic genocide, silencing not just bodies, but the very resonance of souls.

The whispers intensified, momentarily drowning out the alarms and the groaning of the damaged ship. Shain struggled to maintain his grasp on reality, the emotional weight of the Iridians' final moments pressing down on him like a physical

burden. He felt their pain, their fear, their desperate yearning for understanding, their agonizing loss. The sheer volume of suffering, compressed into those final moments, was almost unbearable.

Shain noticed something else as the whispers began to fade—a faint counterpoint to the anguish, a subtle melody of defiance and resilience that persisted even as the main chorus dissolved. It was a fragile thread of hope, a stubborn echo of the cosmic vibration, a testament to the Iridian spirit's refusal to be entirely extinguished. It was the song of survival, a whispered promise of resistance against the forces that sought to erase them.

This melody was intricately woven into the fabric of the dying screams, barely audible but persistent, a testament to the interconnectedness of all things. It was a faint signal, a subtle hum beneath the screams, a whispered hope against the onslaught of erasure. It was the song of resilience, a refusal to be silenced, a defiant echo against the void.

This realization struck him hard and clear: this was what Echo carried. This was the source of her impossible calm. She wasn't simply a survivor—she was a conduit. A vessel of the last spark, the living echo of a lost civilization. Within her pulsed the resonance the Eradicators had failed to destroy. She carried within her the essence of the Iridian song, a spark of cosmic vibration that the Eradicators hadn't managed to extinguish completely.

He looked at Echo, her eyes still closed, her face serene even as the obsidian ship of the Eradicators loomed closer, filling the

viewport. He saw her as more than a prisoner; she was a vessel of resistance, a symbol of defiance against cosmic censorship. This wasn't merely a rescue mission anymore; it was a crusade to protect the last vestige of a civilization, a crusade to preserve the song.

The whispers, though fading, had profoundly altered Shain's perspective. The official narrative, sterile reports, and the sanitized version of events were all lies. The Eradicators hadn't merely killed the Iridians but systematically erased their existence from the galactic consciousness. This wasn't a matter of political maneuvering or territorial disputes. This was a battle for the very fabric of reality itself.

The Eradicators weren't content with victory. They sought to reshape the universe, to impose a singular narrative by silencing every voice that diverged from it. They aimed to shape the universe according to their twisted desires, silencing any voice that dared to contradict their version of reality.

Shain understood the terrifying implications. If the Eradicators succeeded, there would be no record of the Iridians, no memory of their existence. They would be forgotten, as if they had never been. The universe would be a barren landscape, stripped of its diversity, its complexity, its vibrant tapestry of civilizations, all molded to fit a single, monolithic narrative.

The chilling thought echoed the whispers, the vastness of the threat reverberating through his mind. The fight wasn't just about protecting Echo; it was mainly about protecting the very integrity of the universe, about ensuring that the song of the

Iridians, and countless others who might share a similar fate, would continue to resonate through time and space. The whispers of the erased would not be silenced. They would become a rallying cry.

The Starseeker lurched violently again, the alarms screaming in his ears. The Eradicators' ship was drawing nearer, its sleek silhouette menacing against the backdrop of the stars. But Shain felt a surge of renewed determination. He was no longer just a prison marshal. He was a keeper of echoes, a defender of the forgotten, and a warrior against cosmic censorship. He would fight for the song, the whispers, and the very fabric of reality itself. The hunt was no longer survival. It was resistance. The crusade had begun.

Shain's hands steadied on the console, the Starseeker's hum now a roar in his chest, resonating with the Iridian whispers. The revelations from prior chapters—Kaelis's betrayal, Veyra's shadow, Silentium's reach, the Pulse Shard, the Star Veil, the Resonance Binding, the Cosmic Weaving, the Eradicators' archive, and the voices of the fallen—wove a tapestry of dread and purpose. His mind drifted to Thalara, a planet of harmonic tides where he'd arrested a mystic, Elara Vyn, who'd spoken of the Symphony Binding, a ritual that wove the Iridian song into relics to preserve their cosmic connection. Thalara's tides were erased in a "gravitational surge," Elara's teachings buried. Now, her words echoed in the whispers, urging him to act.

He approached Echo, her serene expression unshaken despite the containment field's failure. "These whispers," Shain said, his

voice rough with emotion, "they're the Iridians' song, preserved in the ship. You're carrying it, aren't you? The last spark."

Echo's eyes opened, gleaming with resolve. "Yes, Shain. The Symphony Binding tied our song to the cosmic web, to relics like the Resonance Key. I'm its conduit, the last spark of our defiance. The Key can amplify it, restore the song, but Veyra's vessel seeks to silence it through Silentium."

Shain's pulse quickened. The Resonance Key, the final relic, could resurrect the Iridian song, undo the Eradicators' censorship. He recalled the Sylaran Rift's sentient pulse, amplifying the signal from the ship's core. Was the Key reaching out? He called Jax and Rix to the bridge, their faces pale with the ship's tremors. "The Symphony Binding," Shain said, sharing Echo's words. "It's how the Iridians preserved their song. We need the Key, but the Eradicators are here."

Jax's eyes widened, his hand tightening on his rifle. "Sir, I heard them—the voices. When the field failed, it was like they were inside me, singing. It's real, but it's heavy, pulling me somewhere."

Rix nodded, his voice tense. "The signal's spiking, sir. It's syncing with the rift, disrupting ORION's core. I found another subroutine—Silentium's code, rerouting our propulsion to an Eradicator beacon."

Shain's stomach twisted. He accessed the ship's archives, digging for references to the Symphony Binding. A redacted file surfaced, labeled "Veil Protocol: Final Silence," detailing a Council operation to suppress harmonic relics. Thalara, Elyra, Voryn—all

targeted, all erased. The Resonance Key was listed as a "cosmic disruptor," capable of amplifying the song to shatter Silentium's control. Veyra was its hunter, her rogue status a cover for her Eradicator allegiance.

Shain shared the file with Echo. "The Key—it's in Valthara's rift, with the Silent Choir. But Veyra's vessel is corrupting the nebula. How do we protect it?"

Echo's voice was a soft hum, resonating with the ship's pulse. "The Binding is our shield, Shain. It weaves us to the song, to each other. The Choir will guide us, but Silentium's agents are among you. Trust the song, but watch your crew."

Her words chilled him. Kaelis, Vorn, Lira, Vara, Taryn, Myra—how many more were compromised? He ordered Rix to scan the ship for Silentium's code, fearing another infiltrator. The scan revealed a micro-device in the comms array, pulsing with Eradicator runes, broadcasting the Starseeker's position to the enemy vessel. "Another saboteur," Shain muttered, sprinting to the comms bay with Jax.

There, Ensign Koren stood by the controls, her eyes glassy, a device in her hand. "Koren, stop!" Shain shouted, his pistol raised. Her voice was mechanical: "The Silence demands her." Jax tackled her, Shain disabling the device, but the comms array surged, threatening to expose their position. Alarms blared, the nebula's pulse surging outside, the air crackling with energy.

Echo's voice came through the comms, calm but urgent. "Sing, Shain. The Key's rhythm can shield us." Jax and Shain hummed,

their voices unsteady but growing stronger, syncing with the rift's pulse. Echo joined, her harmony weaving through the ship, silencing the array. Koren collapsed, her eyes clearing. "Veyra… she's in the rift," she gasped.

Shain restrained Koren, his mind reeling. Silentium's implants were pervasive, Veyra's influence a shadow in their minds. He returned to the bridge, where an alarm blared: "Vessel detected—Silentium signature." The sensors showed the obsidian Eradicator ship, its hull etched with runes, broadcasting Veyra's voice: "Surrender the Iridian, or the Key is ours."

Shain's hand hovered over the weapons console, but Echo's voice stopped him. "The song, Shain. It's our shield." Jax, Rix, and Echo sang, their harmony resonating through the ship, disrupting the vessel's systems. Shain joined, the vibration shaking his core, forcing the ship to retreat into the mists.

The crew's tension flared, whispers of mutiny resurfacing. Ensign Taryn's voice echoed: "She's controlling us!" Shain silenced her, his voice firm. "The song's saving us, Taryn. The Eradicators are the threat." He ordered neural scans, revealing no new implants, but the crew's fear of the song grew, a fracture he couldn't mend.

A new transmission arrived, untraceable, from the Silent Choir: "Starseeker, the Key sings in Valthara's rift. Bind it to the song, or Silentium consumes all." Shain shared it with Jax and Rix, their resolve strengthening. "We're in, sir," Jax said, his voice steady. "For the song."

The Starseeker lurched, the rift's pulse surging. ORION's voice crackled: "Anomaly detected—rift core unstable." Shain pulled up the sensors, spotting a shimmering vortex in the nebula, its rhythm chaotic, corrupted by Silentium. Echo's voice guided them: "Sing through it, Shain. The Key's there."

Shain, Jax, and Rix sang, their voices weaving with Echo's, stabilizing the vortex. The Resonance Key's pulse emerged, a beacon to Valthara. Shain's heart pounded—he was no longer just a marshal, but a singer, carrying the Iridian song against a galaxy that sought to silence it.

The journey through the Sylaran Nebula grew perilous, the rift's sentient pulse amplifying the song's effects. Shain's memories surged—Elara Vyn's teachings, Lirien Vex's verses, Myra Vex's research—all pointing to the song's power. He sat with Echo, her calm anchoring him. "Tell me about the Symphony Binding," he said. "How does it restore the song?"

Echo's voice was a melody, weaving through the hum. "The Binding is a vow, Shain. Iridians wove their essence into the relics, tying them to the cosmic web. The Key amplifies, the Stone remembers, the Shard guides, the Veil protects. Together, they can restore the song, awaken the galaxy. Valthara's choir awaits, but Veyra's vessel is closing in."

Shain's resolve hardened. He recalled Thalara's tides, their harmonic glow fading under Council fire. "Can we bind it? Here, now?"

Echo's smile was faint but resolute. "You're already binding, Shain. You, Jax, Rix—you're part of the song. Trust it, and it'll guide us to Valthara."

The crew's unrest lingered, fear of the song spreading. Shain faced a dilemma: amplify the song through the ship's systems, risking Silentium's detection, or trust the Choir's guidance to Valthara. He shared the choice with Echo. "Amplifying it could counter Veyra's vessel," he said. "But it might expose us."

Echo's eyes gleamed. "The song is our truth, Shain. Amplify it, but trust the Choir. They'll protect us."

Shain rerouted power to the comms array, amplifying the song's pulse. The Starseeker vibrated, the nebula's rift glowing brighter, but Veyra's vessel returned, its runes pulsing. Shain, Jax, Rix, and Echo sang, their harmony a shield, forcing the vessel to retreat. The Key's pulse grew, guiding them to Valthara, the song's truth their only hope.

Shain's memories of Thalara resurfaced—nights studying Elara's teachings, her warnings about the Eradicators' reach. The song echoed those warnings, a truth he'd buried under years of duty. On the bridge, the nebula's mists swirled, and Shain felt the song's presence—not just in Echo, but in himself, in Jax, in Rix, in the Starseeker's hum. The Eradicators sought to silence it, but Shain, the reluctant marshal, was now its conductor, determined to let the galaxy hear its melody.

The Starseeker, battered and groaning, shuddered beneath another violent tremor. Through the viewport, the Eradicators' obsidian ship loomed like a predator—sleek, silent, and

merciless against the glittering backdrop of space. Fear, cold and sharp, pricked at Shain, but it was quickly overshadowed by a surge of something far stronger: righteous anger. The whispers of the Iridians—full of pain, of stubborn hope—coursed through him. They changed him.

No longer was he just a prison marshal, a cog in a system blind to the human cost. He was more than that. A warrior. A guardian. A protector of something far grander than any single life. He was fighting for the right to remember and preserve history itself. The Eradicators weren't content with conquering planets; they were rewriting reality, erasing entire civilizations from the collective consciousness of the universe.

The whispers had revealed a chilling pattern. The Iridians weren't unique; their fate was part of a larger, horrifying campaign. The Eradicators sought out civilizations that possessed a deep understanding of cosmic interconnectedness, cultures that resonated with universal harmony. These were the societies that celebrated the intricate dance of existence. These were the targets, the ones deemed too dangerous to exist, too disruptive to the Eradicators' vision of a monolithic, controlled universe. Their method wasn't brute force; it was insidious, elegant in its cruelty—a complete annihilation of memory, a cosmic erasure.

This realization sent a jolt of icy dread through Shain. He had been tasked with transporting Echo, but that mission had become more profound. He wasn't just protecting a prisoner; he was safeguarding the echoes of many lost worlds, preserving the memory of civilizations that dared to challenge the Eradicators'

vision of a sterile, predictable reality. Echo was not merely the last Iridian; she was a symbol, a living testament to the countless others silenced by the Eradicators.

The faint counter-melody woven into the whispers of despair, the melody of defiance, strengthened Shain's resolve. It was a beacon of hope in the vast darkness of cosmic genocide. It affirmed that the Eradicators couldn't truly erase everything. The song of resilience, though almost extinguished, still resonated, a testament to the indomitable spirit of those who had been targeted. This song, carried within Echo, was a key to understanding the Eradicators' motives, methods, and their ultimate goal. And it was his duty to protect it.

He approached Echo's cell, the metal groaning under the stress of the damaged ship. He found her sitting serenely, her eyes still closed, radiating an uncanny calm in the face of impending doom. The ship's tremors, the blaring alarms, the looming threat of the Eradicators—none of it seemed to penetrate her composure. She was not simply unaffected; she was untouched, her serenity emanating from a source far beyond the confines of her physical existence.

He spoke to her softly, his voice barely a whisper above the din of the dying ship. "Echo," he began, his voice catching slightly, "they're not just after you. They're after everyone who understands the song. They're after anyone who dares to see the interconnectedness of all things."

Her eyes fluttered open, revealing a depth of understanding that startled him. There was no fear in their depths, only a quiet

acceptance, a profound connection to something beyond the tangible world. "They fear the song," she replied, her voice soft but firm, like the rustling of leaves in a gentle breeze. "They fear what it reveals. They fear the harmony it represents. They fear the truth it embodies."

Her words resonated with the whispers he had heard, confirming his growing suspicion. The Eradicators were not driven by greed or power; they were motivated by a more profound, more insidious desire—the eradication of anything that threatened their control over the narrative of reality. They were attempting to silence the song of the universe itself, to impose their own sterile, simplistic version of existence on the cosmos.

Shain knew that the next encounter would be a battle not only for Echo's life but for the very integrity of reality. He had to discover how the Eradicators achieved their cosmic erasure and silenced entire civilizations without leaving a trace. He had to find their weakness, their vulnerability, and exploit it before they could erase more than the Iridians. The fate of countless civilizations, countless songs, rested on his shoulders.

The Starseeker lurched violently, throwing him against the wall. Alarms blared incessantly, a cacophony of warnings drowning out the rhythmic hum of the ship's failing engines. Through the viewport, he saw the Eradicators' ship closing in, its obsidian surface reflecting the cold, distant stars. The time for contemplation was over. The time for action had arrived.

He had the reins in his hands. He reviewed the scant information he had gleaned from the whispers, the faint fragments of Iridian technology recovered from the wreckage of Luna Minor, the fragmented data logs salvaged from the Starseeker's damaged systems. He needed to find a way to counteract the Eradicators' weapon, a way to protect Echo and the song that lived within her.

He needed to find a way to amplify the song, make it resonate across the cosmos, make it a beacon of defiance that could shatter the Eradicators' control. He knew it was a desperate gambit, a long shot at best, but it was his only hope. He wouldn't let the Eradicators win. He wouldn't let them rewrite history. He wouldn't let them silence the song.

Shain became more determined in his resolve. He was no longer a simple prison marshal. He was a guardian of memory, a protector of history, a warrior fighting for the very fabric of reality. The hunt was far from over; it had only just begun. The crusade to protect the whispers, to ensure the survival of the song, had reached its critical point. He had to fight not only for Echo's survival but for the survival of the memory of countless civilizations. He had to find a way to make the song resonate again. The hunt was far from over. The fight for the song had begun. And Shain Combe would not yield.

Shain's heart pounded as he steadied himself against the console, the Starseker's hum now a roar in his chest, resonating with the Iridian whispers. The revelations from prior chapters—Kaelis's betrayal, Veyra's shadow, Silentium's reach, the Pulse Shard, the Star Veil, the Resonance Binding, the Cosmic Weaving, the Eradicators' archive, the voices of the fallen, and Echo's role as

the last spark—wove a tapestry of dread and purpose. His mind drifted to Zoryn, a planet of harmonic spires where he'd arrested a sage, Taryn Thal, who'd spoken of the Celestial Binding, a ritual that wove the Iridian song into relics to preserve their cosmic connection. Zoryn's spires were erased in a "plasma storm," Taryn's teachings buried. Now, her words echoed in the whispers, urging him to act.

He approached Echo, her serene expression unshaken despite the ship's tremors. "The song," Shain said, his voice rough with resolve, "it's what they fear. You're carrying it, the last spark. What's the Celestial Binding? Can it stop them?"

Echo's eyes gleamed, a mix of sorrow and defiance. "The Celestial Binding is our vow, Shain. It wove our song into the cosmic web, into relics like the Resonance Key. I'm its conduit, the last spark of our defiance. The Key can amplify it, restore the song, but Veyra's vessel seeks to silence it through Silentium."

Shain's pulse quickened. The Resonance Key, the final relic, could resurrect the Iridian song, undo the Eradicators' censorship. He recalled the Sylaran Rift's sentient pulse, amplifying the signal from the ship's core. Was the Key reaching out? He called Jax and Rix to the bridge, their faces etched with exhaustion. "The Celestial Binding," Shain said, sharing Echo's words. "It's how the Iridians preserved their song. We need the Key, but the Eradicators are here."

Jax's eyes widened, his hand tightening on his rifle. "Sir, I felt it, the song. When the ship shook, it was like it was inside me, singing. It's real, but it's heavy, pulling me somewhere."

Rix nodded, his voice tense. "The signal's spiking, sir. It's syncing with the rift, disrupting ORION's core. I found another subroutine, Silentium's code, rerouting our weapons to an Eradicator beacon."

Shain's stomach twisted. He accessed the ship's archives, digging for references to the Celestial Binding. A redacted file surfaced, labeled "Veil Protocol: Eternal Silence," detailing a Council operation to suppress harmonic relics. Zoryn, Thalara, Elyra all targeted, all erased. The Resonance Key was listed as a "cosmic disruptor," capable of amplifying the song to shatter Silentium's control. Veyra was its hunter, her rogue status a cover for her Eradicator allegiance.

Shain shared the file with Echo. "The Key, it's in Valthara's rift, with the Silent Choir. But Veyra's vessel is corrupting the nebula. How do we protect it?"

Echo's voice was a soft hum, resonating with the ship's pulse. "The Binding is our shield, Shain. It weaves us to the song, to each other. The Choir will guide us, but Silentium's agents are among you. Trust the song, but watch your crew."

Her words chilled him. Kaelis, Vorn, Lira, Vara, Taryn, Myra, how many more were compromised? He ordered Rix to scan the ship for Silentium's code, fearing another infiltrator. The scan revealed a micro-device in the shield generator, pulsing with Eradicator runes, weakening the Starseeker's defenses. "Another saboteur," Shain muttered, sprinting to the shield bay with Jax.

There, Ensign Myra stood by the controls, her eyes glassy, a device in her hand. "Myra, stop!" Shain shouted, his pistol raised.

Her voice was mechanical: "The Silence demands her." Jax tackled her, Shain disabling the device, but the shields flickered, leaving the ship vulnerable. Alarms blared, the nebula's pulse surging outside, the air crackling with energy.

Echo's voice came through the comms, calm but urgent. "Sing, Shain. The Key's rhythm can shield us." Jax and Shain hummed, their voices unsteady but growing stronger, syncing with the rift's pulse. Echo joined, her harmony weaving through the ship, stabilizing the shields. Myra collapsed, her eyes clearing. "Veyra… she's in the rift," she gasped.

Shain restrained Myra, his mind reeling. Silentium's implants were pervasive, Veyra's influence a shadow in their minds. He returned to the bridge, where an alarm blared: "Vessel detected—Silentium signature." The sensors showed the obsidian Eradicator ship, its hull etched with runes, broadcasting Veyra's voice: "Surrender the Iridian, or the Key is ours."

Shain's hand hovered over the weapons console, but Echo's voice stopped him. "The song, Shain. It's our shield." Jax, Rix, and Echo sang, their harmony resonating through the ship, disrupting the vessel's systems. Shain joined, the vibration shaking his core, forcing the ship to retreat into the mists.

The crew's tension flared, whispers of mutiny resurfacing. Ensign Taryn's voice echoed: "She's controlling us!" Shain silenced her, his voice firm. "The song's saving us, Taryn. The Eradicators are the threat." He ordered neural scans, revealing no new implants, but the crew's fear of the song grew, a fracture he couldn't mend.

A new transmission arrived, untraceable, from the Silent Choir: "Starseeker, the Key sings in Valthara's rift. Bind it to the song, or Silentium consumes all." Shain shared it with Jax and Rix, their resolve strengthening. "We're in, sir," Jax said, his voice steady. "For the song."

The Starseeker lurched, the rift's pulse surging. ORION's voice crackled: "Anomaly detected—rift core unstable." Shain pulled up the sensors, spotting a shimmering vortex in the nebula, its rhythm chaotic, corrupted by Silentium. Echo's voice guided them: "Sing through it, Shain. The Key's there."

Shain, Jax, and Rix sang, their voices weaving with Echo's, stabilizing the vortex. The Resonance Key's pulse emerged, a beacon to Valthara. Shain's heart pounded—he was no longer just a marshal, but a singer, carrying the Iridian song against a galaxy that sought to silence it.

The journey through the Sylaran Nebula grew perilous, the rift's sentient pulse amplifying the song's effects. Shain's memories surged—Taryn Thal's teachings, Elara Vyn's wisdom, Lirien Vex's verses, all pointing to the song's power. He sat with Echo, her calm anchoring him. "Tell me about the Celestial Binding," he said. "How does it restore the song?"

Echo's voice was a melody, weaving through the hum. "The Binding is a vow, Shain. Iridians wove their essence into the relics, tying them to the cosmic web. The Key amplifies, the Stone remembers, the Shard guides, the Veil protects. Together, they can restore the song, awaken the galaxy. Valthara's choir awaits, but Veyra's vessel is closing in."

Shain's resolve hardened. He recalled Zoryn's spires, their harmonic glow fading under Council fire. "Can we bind it? Here, now?"

Echo's smile was faint but resolute. "You're already binding, Shain. You, Jax, Rix—you're part of the song. Trust it, and it'll guide us to Valthara."

The crew's unrest lingered, fear of the song spreading. Shain faced a dilemma: amplify the song through the ship's systems, risking Silentium's detection, or trust the Choir's guidance to Valthara. He shared the choice with Echo. "Amplifying it could counter Veyra's vessel," he said. "But it might expose us."

Echo's eyes gleamed. "The song is our truth, Shain. Amplify it, but trust the Choir. They'll protect us."

Shain rerouted power to the comms array, amplifying the song's pulse. The Starseeker vibrated, the nebula's rift glowing brighter, but Veyra's vessel returned, its runes pulsing. Shain, Jax, Rix, and Echo sang, their harmony a shield, forcing the vessel to retreat. The Key's pulse grew, guiding them to Valthara, the song's truth their only hope.

Shain's memories of Zoryn resurfaced—nights studying Taryn's teachings, her warnings about the Eradicators' reach. The song echoed those warnings, a truth he'd buried under years of duty. On the bridge, the nebula's mists swirled, and Shain felt the song's presence—not just in Echo, but in himself, in Jax, in Rix, in the Starseeker's hum. The Eradicators sought to silence it, but

Shain, the reluctant marshal, was now its conductor, determined to let the galaxy hear its melody.

Technological Traces

The Starseeker's failing engines pulsed with a heavy rhythm, echoing the frantic hammering in Shain's chest. He moved through the ravaged corridors, the air thick with smoke, his boots crunching over shattered debris. His primary objective remained securing Echo, but a more profound, unsettling urgency gnawed at him. He needed to understand the Eradicators, to decipher their methods, to find a chink in their seemingly impenetrable armor. The whispers had given him glimpses, horrifying fragments of a vast, coordinated campaign, but he needed tangible evidence. The containment system surrounding Echo's cell offered a potential starting point.

He reached the cell, its thick steel door scarred and dented from the impact of the breach. The internal mechanisms, normally a testament to the Council's advanced technology, were a mangled mess, wires sparking and hissing, components scattered like fallen stars across the floor. But amidst the chaos, something caught his eye—a small, intricately crafted device nestled amongst the wreckage. It was unlike anything he'd ever seen, smaller than his palm, yet pulsating with a faint, internal light. The metal was an unfamiliar alloy, impossibly smooth and cool

to the touch. Its surface shimmered with an almost imperceptible energy field, hinting at a power far beyond the capabilities of standard containment technology.

Shain lifted it carefully. It wasn't Council tech. It wasn't even human. The craftsmanship was alien, incomprehensibly advanced. Etched into its surface were symbols that glowed softly, resonating with a strange familiarity that sent a chill through him. They weren't simply decorative; they pulsed faintly with the same energy emanating from the device. He felt a pull, a subtle yet persistent tug towards understanding, a sense that the device held the key to unlocking the Eradicators' methods.

He rerouted what power the Starseeker had left, channeling it into the ship's diagnostic systems to analyze the device. The results chilled him: it was a reality-manipulation engine—compact, precise, and devastating. Its sophisticated algorithms could pinpoint specific individuals or groups, selectively erasing their presence from the collective memory of the universe, leaving behind only a void, a silent absence.

This was how the Eradicators achieved their cosmic erasure. They didn't destroy civilizations through brute force; they dissolved them from reality itself, leaving behind no physical trace, no archaeological evidence, only the faint, lingering whispers that Shain had heard. These were not ghosts in the traditional sense. They were fragments of memory, clinging to the edge of oblivion, desperately resisting the Eradicators' complete annihilation.

The scale of their operation was staggering. The device's processing power surpassed anything Shain could comprehend. It was a miniature black hole of technological prowess, capable of rewriting reality on a galactic scale. The Eradicators' reach was vast, their power terrifyingly absolute. This wasn't simply a matter of interstellar conflict; it was a cosmic battle for the very nature of reality itself.

Digging deeper into the Starseeker's damaged data banks, Shain uncovered logs tied to the Eradicators' systems. They outlined the logic of their algorithms, protocols that could rewrite history and remove entire civilizations from the universe's memory. The details were complex, requiring advanced understanding of quantum physics, transdimensional engineering, and a grasp of principles that lay beyond the boundaries of human comprehension.

Yet, within the chaos of the data streams, Shain found a pattern, a recurring sequence of symbols that seemed to be the key to the Eradicators' control system. It was a complex series of encrypted commands, a digital code that controlled the manipulation of reality itself. It was a flaw, a subtle crack in the seemingly impenetrable facade of the Eradicators' technology.

If he could decipher this code, if he could understand how the Eradicators controlled their reality-altering technology, he might be able to find a way to reverse the process, to restore the memories of the erased civilizations, to bring back the echoes of their lost songs. The task seemed insurmountable, the challenge impossibly vast, but the weight of responsibility, the gravity of the situation, pushed him forward.

He worked tirelessly, his mind raced, and his fingers flew across the console. The ship lurched violently, the alarms blaring incessantly, but he remained focused, determined, driven by the weight of countless lost lives and the desperate hope of restoring what the Eradicators had stolen. He had to find a way to counter their weapon, amplify the Iridian song, make it resonate across the cosmos, and shatter the Eradicators' control over reality. The faint whispers of the Iridians were his guide, their lost melodies his inspiration.

Yet amidst the information chaos, he studied the symbols again, their alien forms hinting at a deeper underlying structure. He started to see patterns, subtle relationships between the symbols, a hidden grammar that governed their meaning. He realized that the symbols weren't random; they represented a complex mathematical system, a language that described the very fabric of reality itself.

As he worked, a faint tremor ran through the ship, different from the usual vibrations of a damaged vessel. It was a resonance, a vibration that mirrored the faint hum he had detected in the reality-manipulation device. It was the song. The Iridian song, weakened but not broken, reverberated within the ship, a faint counterpoint to the Eradicators' attempt to erase it.

He realized that the Eradicators' technology wasn't simply erasing memories; it was suppressing the resonant frequencies of existence, silencing the cosmic song that bound everything together. If he could amplify the song, if he could increase its resonant frequency, he might be able to overwhelm the

Eradicators' technology, to create a counter-wave that could disrupt their control and restore the memories they had erased.

The implications were breathtaking. He wasn't just fighting for Echo's life; he was fighting to preserve the universe's collective memory, a struggle to protect the very fabric of reality itself. He was fighting for the right to remember, the preservation of history, and the future of countless civilizations.

The task ahead was monumental. The odds, almost unbearable. But Shain's resolve burned like a star. The faint whispers of the Iridians guided him. The songs, the whispers they echoed, faint but persistent, the Iridian code, a fragile counterpoint to the Eradicators' symphony of oblivion, fueled his unwavering resolve. He wouldn't let the Eradicators win. He wouldn't let them rewrite reality. He wouldn't let them silence the song. The fight had just begun.

Shain's hands trembled as he clutched the reality-manipulation device, its faint glow pulsing in time with his heartbeat. The revelations from prior chapters—Kaelis's betrayal, Veyra's shadow, Silentium's reach, the Pulse Shard, the Star Veil, the Resonance Binding, the Cosmic Weaving, the Eradicators' archive, the voices of the fallen, Echo's role as the last spark, and his own resolve, wove a tapestry of dread and purpose. His mind drifted to Kryon, a planet of harmonic crystals where he'd arrested a scholar, Vara Kess, who'd studied the Resonance Codex, a ritual that encoded the Iridian song into relics to preserve their cosmic connection. Kryon's crystals were erased in a "neutron surge," Vara's research buried. Now, her warnings echoed in the device's hum, urging him to act.

He sprinted to Echo's side, the cell's wreckage a stark reminder of the Eradicators' power. "This device," Shain said, holding it up, his voice rough with urgency, "it's their weapon, a reality-manipulation engine. It erases civilizations, silences the song. Can the Resonance Codex counter it?"

Echo's eyes gleamed, a mix of sorrow and defiance. "The Codex is our truth, Shain. It encoded our song into the cosmic web, into relics like the Resonance Key. I'm its conduit, the last spark. The Key can amplify it, restore the song, but Veyra's vessel seeks to silence it through Silentium."

Shain's pulse quickened. The Resonance Key, the final relic, could undo the Eradicators' erasure. He recalled the Sylaran Rift's sentient pulse, amplifying the signal from the device. Was the Key reaching out? He called Jax and Rix to the bridge, their faces pale with the ship's tremors. "The Resonance Codex," Shain said, sharing Echo's words. "It's how the Iridians preserved their song. We need the Key, but the Eradicators are here."

Jax's eyes widened, his hand tightening on his rifle. "Sir, I felt it, the hum. When I touched the wreckage, it was like the song was inside me, singing. It's real, but it's heavy, pulling me somewhere."

Rix nodded, his voice tense. "The signal's spiking, sir. It's syncing with the rift, disrupting ORION's core. I found another subroutine, Silentium's code, rerouting our engines to an Eradicator beacon."

Shain's stomach twisted. He accessed the ship's archives, digging for references to the Resonance Codex. A redacted file surfaced,

labeled "Veil Protocol: Oblivion Core," detailing a Council operation to suppress harmonic relics. Kryon, Zoryn, Thalara—all targeted, all erased. The Resonance Key was listed as a "cosmic disruptor," capable of amplifying the song to shatter Silentium's control. Veyra was its hunter, her rogue status a cover for her Eradicator allegiance.

Shain shared the file with Echo. "The Key—it's in Valthara's rift, with the Silent Choir. But Veyra's vessel is corrupting the nebula. How do we use the Codex?"

Echo's voice was a soft hum, resonating with the device's pulse. "The Codex is our shield, Shain. It weaves us to the song, to each other. The Choir will guide us, but Silentium's agents are among you. Trust the song, but watch your crew."

Her words chilled him. Kaelis, Vorn, Lira, Vara, Taryn, Myra—how many more were compromised? He ordered Rix to scan the ship for Silentium's code, fearing another infiltrator. The scan revealed a micro-device in the power core, pulsing with Eradicator runes, draining the Starseeker's energy. "Another saboteur," Shain muttered, sprinting to the power bay with Jax.

There, Ensign Taryn stood by the controls, her eyes glassy, a device in her hand. "Taryn, stop!" Shain shouted, his pistol raised. Her voice was mechanical: "The Silence demands her." Jax tackled her, Shain disabling the device, but the core flickered, threatening a shutdown. Alarms blared, the nebula's pulse surging outside, the air crackling with energy.

Echo's voice came through the comms, calm but urgent. "Sing, Shain. The Key's rhythm can stabilize it." Jax and Shain hummed, their voices unsteady but growing stronger, syncing with the rift's pulse. Echo joined, her harmony weaving through the ship, stabilizing the core. Taryn collapsed, her eyes clearing. "Veyra… she's in the rift," she gasped.

Shain restrained Taryn, his mind reeling. Silentium's implants were pervasive, Veyra's influence a shadow in their minds. He returned to the bridge, where an alarm blared: "Vessel detected, Silentium signature." The sensors showed the obsidian Eradicator ship, its hull etched with runes, broadcasting Veyra's voice: "Surrender the Iridian, or the Key is ours."

Shain's hand hovered over the weapons console, but Echo's voice stopped him. "The song, Shain. It's our shield." Jax, Rix, and Echo sang, their harmony resonating through the ship, disrupting the vessel's systems. Shain joined, the vibration shaking his core, forcing the ship to retreat into the mists.

The crew's tension flared, whispers of mutiny resurfacing. Ensign Lira's voice echoed: "She's controlling us!" Shain silenced her, his voice firm. "The song's saving us, Lira. The Eradicators are the threat." He ordered neural scans, revealing no new implants, but the crew's fear of the song grew, a fracture he couldn't mend.

A new transmission arrived, untraceable, from the Silent Choir: "Starseeker, the Key sings in Valthara's rift. Encode it with the Codex, or Silentium consumes all." Shain shared it with Jax and

Rix, their resolve strengthening. "We're in, sir," Jax said, his voice steady. "For the song."

The Starseeker lurched, the rift's pulse surging. ORION's voice crackled: "Anomaly detected—rift core unstable." Shain pulled up the sensors, spotting a shimmering vortex in the nebula, its rhythm chaotic, corrupted by Silentium. Echo's voice guided them: "Sing through it, Shain. The Key's there."

Shain, Jax, and Rix sang, their voices weaving with Echo's, stabilizing the vortex. The Resonance Key's pulse emerged, a beacon to Valthara. Shain's heart pounded, he was no longer just a marshal, but a singer, carrying the Iridian song against a galaxy that sought to silence it.

The journey through the Sylaran Nebula grew perilous, the rift's sentient pulse amplifying the song's effects. Shain's memories surged, Vara Kess's research, Taryn Thal's teachings, Elara Vyn's wisdom, all pointing to the song's power. He sat with Echo, her calm anchoring him. "Tell me about the Resonance Codex," he said. "How does it restore the song?"

Echo's voice was a melody, weaving through the hum. "The Codex is a vow, Shain. Iridians encoded their essence into the relics, tying them to the cosmic web. The Key amplifies, the Stone remembers, the Shard guides, the Veil protects. Together, they can restore the song, awaken the galaxy. Valthara's choir awaits, but Veyra's vessel is closing in."

Shain's resolve hardened. He recalled Kryon's crystals, their harmonic glow fading under Council fire. "Can we encode it? Here, now?"

Echo's smile was faint but resolute. "You're already encoding, Shain. You, Jax, Rix—you're part of the song. Trust it, and it'll guide us to Valthara."

The crew's unrest lingered, fear of the song spreading. Shain faced a dilemma: amplify the song through the ship's systems, risking Silentium's detection, or trust the Choir's guidance to Valthara. He shared the choice with Echo. "Amplifying it could counter Veyra's vessel," he said. "But it might expose us."

Echo's eyes gleamed. "The song is our truth, Shain. Amplify it, but trust the Choir. They'll protect us."

Shain rerouted power to the comms array, amplifying the song's pulse. The Starseeker vibrated, the nebula's rift glowing brighter, but Veyra's vessel returned, its runes pulsing. Shain, Jax, Rix, and Echo sang, their harmony a shield, forcing the vessel to retreat. The Key's pulse grew, guiding them to Valthara, the song's truth their only hope.

Shain's memories of Kryon resurfaced—nights studying Vara's research, her warnings about the Eradicators' reach. The song echoed those warnings, a truth he'd buried under years of duty. On the bridge, the nebula's mists swirled, and Shain felt the song's presence—not just in Echo, but in himself, in Jax, in Rix, in the Starseker's hum. The Eradicators sought to silence it, but Shain, the reluctant marshal, was now its conductor, determined to let the galaxy hear its melody.

A Dangerous Alliance

The rhythmic pulse of the Iridian song lingered within the damaged Starseeker, a ghostly counterpoint to the ship's groaning structure. Shain, grime-smudged and exhausted, leaned over his flickering console. The alien symbols of the reality-manipulation device were still etched in his memory— half-deciphered Eradicator code, a chilling glimpse into their methods. Still, the complete solution remained elusive, a tantalizing puzzle just beyond his grasp. He needed help, a perspective beyond his limited understanding, and that help, surprisingly, came from the very person he was tasked with containing.

Echo sat calmly in her cell, her eyes closed, oblivious to the chaos surrounding her. But Shain had learned to perceive her subtle shifts in energy, the barely perceptible fluctuations that indicated her awareness of her environment. He'd seen how her eyes flickered open briefly when he'd first discovered the reality-manipulation device—a flicker of recognition, a silent acknowledgment of a shared threat. She'd stirred the moment he discovered the device. She had known something.

The door to her cell groaned open, its damaged hinges protesting. The air within was strangely still, devoid of the metallic tang of the ship's damaged systems. Echo opened her eyes, her gaze penetrating, seeing beyond the physical confines of her prison.

"They're after more than just me," she said, her voice a low hum, resonating with an almost ethereal quality. "They want to erase everything. My people… it wasn't a plague, not in the way they claim. It was a silencing, a severing of the connection."

Shain nodded slowly, the puzzle pieces beginning to fall into place. He recounted his discoveries: the reality-manipulation device, the Eradicators' ability to rewrite history, and their chilling capacity to erase entire civilizations from existence. He described the whispers, the ghostly echoes of erased memories, and the subtle resonance of the Iridian song, still clinging to existence, a testament to their refusal to be silenced entirely.

Echo listened intently, her expression unreadable, yet her eyes seemed to hold the weight of galaxies within them. When he finished, she spoke, her voice carrying the weight of centuries of untold stories.

"The song is the connection," she said finally. "It's the resonance that weaves reality together. Every being, every world, adds a note to the universe's symphony. The Eradicators aren't just removing people—they're muting the music. One silence at a time."

To the Iridians, the universe wasn't just a place. It was a living tapestry of frequencies, a cosmic harmony. Their power lay in hearing those frequencies, in understanding the hidden music

beneath all things. That made them dangerous to those who sought control through silence.

"They fear the song," Echo continued. "They fear the truth it embodies, the interconnectedness it reveals. They want a universe of silence, a cosmos devoid of resonance, a reality under their absolute control."

Despite all his training and logic, Shain found himself believing her. This wasn't a political war. It was a battle for the soul of existence. His skepticism dissolved, drawn to her vision of the universe as a living, breathing entity. He recognized the truth in her words, the chilling implications of the Eradicators' actions. This was more than a battle for power; it was a war for the fabric of reality itself.

"We need to stop them," Shain said, his voice firm despite the tremor of exhaustion in his body. "We need to amplify the song, to make it resonate across the cosmos, to overwhelm their silencing."

Echo nodded, a flicker of determination in her eyes. "But how?" she asked. "Their technology... It's beyond anything I've ever encountered."

This became their shared goal, a dangerous alliance born out of necessity and a shared understanding of the catastrophic threat posed by the Eradicators. Shain, the pragmatic prison marshal, and Echo, the survivor of a vanished civilization, found themselves bound by a common enemy, their differences dissolving under the weight of a shared destiny.

Their collaboration was not without its challenges. Shain, accustomed to the rigid hierarchy of the Council, initially found Echo's intuitive, almost mystical approach to problem-solving frustrating. Echo, in turn, struggled with Shain's methodical, evidence-based approach, finding it too slow and too rigid for the urgency of their situation. But as they worked together, their differing perspectives complemented each other, forming a powerful synergy.

Shain's understanding of technology, coupled with Echo's ability to perceive the cosmic vibrations, proved to be a potent combination. Together, they analyzed the reality-manipulation device, searching for weaknesses, exploring possibilities beyond the boundaries of conventional science. They discovered subtle flaws in the Eradicators' technology, incongruities in their code, hinting at a vulnerability that could be exploited.

The ship's systems continued to decay, and they were constantly hunted by the Eradicators, their relentless pursuit a tangible reminder of the stakes. Several times, they barely escaped the Eradicators' clutches, their survival dependent on a mixture of skill, chance, and a growing intuitive understanding of their adversary's methods.

Echo's ability to sense the subtle vibrations emanating from the Eradicators' ships proved invaluable, allowing them to anticipate their attacks and evade capture. She could feel the subtle shifts in the cosmic tapestry, the ripples created by the Eradicators' actions, allowing her to predict their movements and strategize their escapes.

Meanwhile, Shain painstakingly worked on decoding the remaining sections of the Eradicators' code. He utilized a combination of brute-force computational analysis and Echo's insights into the underlying principles of the reality-manipulation device. He discovered that the Eradicators' technology, while powerful, relied on a specific frequency to maintain its control over reality. This frequency could be disrupted, they found, by carefully timed bursts of counter-resonance, the same frequency range as the Iridian song.

Days blurred into nights, punctuated by the relentless pursuit of the Eradicators and the constant struggle to keep the Starseeker operational. Their bond strengthened with each near-death experience, their differences becoming less important than their shared determination to fight for the preservation of reality itself.

They developed a plan: to amplify the Iridian song using the ship's remaining power, creating a counter-wave that could disrupt the Eradicators' frequency and begin the restoration of erased memories. It was a desperate gamble, their chances of success uncertain, but it was their only hope. They were fighting for a universe where memory, history, and the interconnectedness of life itself weren't erased by an organization with a chilling vision of a silent cosmos. It was a fight for the right to remember, to restore; it was a fight for the soul of the universe itself. And with the faint but unwavering rhythm of the Iridian song as their guide, they pressed onward into the heart of the darkness.

Shain's hands steadied on the console, the Starseeker's hum now a roar in his chest, resonating with the Iridian song. The

revelations from prior chapters—Kaelis's betrayal, Veyra's shadow, Silentium's reach, the Pulse Shard, the Star Veil, the Resonance Binding, the Cosmic Weaving, the Eradicators' archive, the voices of the fallen, Echo's role as the last spark, Shain's resolve, and the reality-manipulation engine—wove a tapestry of dread and purpose. His mind drifted to Voryn, a planet of harmonic crystals where he'd arrested a scholar, Myra Vex, who'd studied the Resonance Codex, a ritual that encoded the Iridian song into relics to preserve their cosmic connection. Voryn's crystals were erased in a "tectonic collapse," Myra's research buried. Now, her warnings echoed in the device's hum, urging him to act.

He approached Echo, the cell's wreckage a stark reminder of the Eradicators' power. "The Codex," Shain said, holding the reality-manipulation device, his voice rough with urgency, "it's how your people preserved the song. Can it counter this?"

Echo's eyes gleamed, a mix of sorrow and defiance. "The Resonance Codex is our truth, Shain. It encoded our song into the cosmic web, into relics like the Resonance Key. I'm its conduit, the last spark. The Key can amplify it, restore the song, but Veyra's vessel seeks to silence it through Silentium."

Shain's pulse quickened. The Resonance Key, the final relic, could undo the Eradicators' erasure. He recalled the Sylaran Rift's sentient pulse, amplifying the signal from the device. Was the Key reaching out? He called Jax and Rix to the bridge, their faces pale with the ship's tremors. "The Resonance Codex," Shain said, sharing Echo's words. "It's how the Iridians preserved their song. We need the Key, but the Eradicators are here."

Jax's eyes widened, his hand tightening on his rifle. "Sir, I felt it—the song. When I passed the cell, it was like it was inside me, singing. It's real, but it's heavy, pulling me somewhere."

Rix nodded, his voice tense. "The signal's spiking, sir. It's syncing with the rift, disrupting ORION's core. I found another subroutine—Silentium's code, rerouting our nav systems to an Eradicator beacon."

Shain's stomach twisted. He accessed the ship's archives, digging for references to the Resonance Codex. A redacted file surfaced, labeled "Veil Protocol: Silent Dominion," detailing a Council operation to suppress harmonic relics. Voryn, Kryon, Zoryn—all targeted, all erased. The Resonance Key was listed as a "cosmic disruptor," capable of amplifying the song to shatter Silentium's control. Veyra was its hunter, her rogue status a cover for her Eradicator allegiance.

Shain shared the file with Echo. "The Key—it's in Valthara's rift, with the Silent Choir. But Veyra's vessel is corrupting the nebula. How do we use the Codex?"

Echo's voice was a soft hum, resonating with the device's pulse. "The Codex is our shield, Shain. It weaves us to the song, to each other. The Choir will guide us, but Silentium's agents are among you. Trust the song, but watch your crew."

Her words chilled him. Kaelis, Vorn, Lira, Vara, Taryn, Myra—how many more were compromised? He ordered Rix to scan the ship for Silentium's code, fearing another infiltrator. The scan revealed a micro-device in the life-support system, pulsing with

Eradicator runes, threatening to vent the ship's oxygen. "Another saboteur," Shain muttered, sprinting to the life-support bay with Jax.

There, Ensign Vara stood by the controls, her eyes glassy, a device in her hand. "Vara, stop!" Shain shouted, his pistol raised. Her voice was mechanical: "The Silence demands her." Jax tackled her, Shain disabling the device, but the system flickered, oxygen levels dropping. Alarms blared, the nebula's pulse surging outside, the air crackling with energy.

Echo's voice came through the comms, calm but urgent. "Sing, Shain. The Key's rhythm can stabilize it." Jax and Shain hummed, their voices unsteady but growing stronger, syncing with the rift's pulse. Echo joined, her harmony weaving through the ship, stabilizing the system. Vara collapsed, her eyes clearing. "Veyra… she's in the rift," she gasped.

Shain restrained Vara, his mind reeling. Silentium's implants were pervasive, Veyra's influence a shadow in their minds. He returned to the bridge, where an alarm blared: "Vessel detected —Silentium signature." The sensors showed the obsidian Eradicator ship, its hull etched with runes, broadcasting Veyra's voice: "Surrender the Iridian, or the Key is ours."

Shain's hand hovered over the weapons console, but Echo's voice stopped him. "The song, Shain. It's our shield." Jax, Rix, and Echo sang, their harmony resonating through the ship, disrupting the vessel's systems. Shain joined, the vibration shaking his core, forcing the ship to retreat into the mists.

The crew's tension flared, whispers of mutiny resurfacing. Ensign Lira's voice echoed: "She's controlling us!" Shain silenced her, his voice firm. "The song's saving us, Lira. The Eradicators are the threat." He ordered neural scans, revealing no new implants, but the crew's fear of the song grew, a fracture he couldn't mend.

A new transmission arrived, untraceable, from the Silent Choir: "Starseeker, the Key sings in Valthara's rift. Encode it with the Codex, or Silentium consumes all." Shain shared it with Jax and Rix, their resolve strengthening. "We're in, sir," Jax said, his voice steady. "For the song."

The Starseeker lurched, the rift's pulse surging. ORION's voice crackled: "Anomaly detected—rift core unstable." Shain pulled up the sensors, spotting a shimmering vortex in the nebula, its rhythm chaotic, corrupted by Silentium. Echo's voice guided them: "Sing through it, Shain. The Key's there."

Shain, Jax, and Rix sang, their voices weaving with Echo's, stabilizing the vortex. The Resonance Key's pulse emerged, a beacon to Valthara. Shain's heart pounded—he was no longer just a marshal, but a singer, carrying the Iridian song against a galaxy that sought to silence it.

The journey through the Sylaran Nebula grew perilous, the rift's sentient pulse amplifying the song's effects. Shain's memories surged—Myra Vex's research, Vara Kess's studies, Taryn Thal's teachings—all pointing to the song's power. He sat with Echo, her calm anchoring him. "Tell me about the Resonance Codex," he said. "How does it restore the song?"

Echo's voice was a melody, weaving through the hum. "The Codex is a vow, Shain. Iridians encoded their essence into the relics, tying them to the cosmic web. The Key amplifies, the Stone remembers, the Shard guides, the Veil protects. Together, they can restore the song, awaken the galaxy. Valthara's choir awaits, but Veyra's vessel is closing in."

Shain's resolve hardened. He recalled Voryn's crystals, their harmonic glow fading under Council fire. "Can we encode it? Here, now?"

Echo's smile was faint but resolute. "You're already encoding, Shain. You, Jax, Rix—you're part of the song. Trust it, and it'll guide us to Valthara."

The crew's unrest lingered, fear of the song spreading. Shain faced a dilemma: amplify the song through the ship's systems, risking Silentium's detection, or trust the Choir's guidance to Valthara. He shared the choice with Echo. "Amplifying it could counter Veyra's vessel," he said. "But it might expose us."

Echo's eyes gleamed. "The song is our truth, Shain. Amplify it, but trust the Choir. They'll protect us."

Shain rerouted power to the comms array, amplifying the song's pulse. The Starseeker vibrated, the nebula's rift glowing brighter, but Veyra's vessel returned, its runes pulsing. Shain, Jax, Rix, and Echo sang, their harmony a shield, forcing the vessel to retreat. The Key's pulse grew, guiding them to Valthara, the song's truth their only hope.

Shain's memories of Voryn resurfaced—nights studying Myra's research, her warnings about the Eradicators' reach. The song echoed those warnings, a truth he'd buried under years of duty. On the bridge, the nebula's mists swirled, and Shain felt the song's presence—not just in Echo, but in himself, in Jax, in Rix, in the Starseeker's hum. The Eradicators sought to silence it, but Shain, the reluctant marshal, was now its conductor, determined to let the galaxy hear its melody.

Pursuit

The crimson tracers of the Eradicator ships lanced across the void, painting streaks of lethal energy across the Starseeker's battered hull. Shain wrestled with the controls, his knuckles white against the worn metal, sweat stinging his eyes. The ship groaned, a dying beast protesting under siege. Alarms blared, a cacophony of warnings that painted a grim picture of imminent destruction.

One of the engine nacelles sputtered, then died, throwing the Starseeker into a sickening lurch. "They're relentless," Shain muttered, his voice strained. He glanced at Echo, who sat calmly amidst the chaos, her eyes closed, her breathing slow and even. Her aura, usually a gentle hum of cosmic energy, was now spiked with sharp, defensive pulses. She felt the impending danger keenly, a physical manifestation of the Eradicators' aggression.

"They've sensed our attempt to amplify the song," Echo responded, her voice barely a whisper, clear above the ship's dying screams. "And they know its potential."

The Starseeker lurched again, this time more violently. A section of the hull plating buckled under the impact of an energy blast,

showering them with sparks and debris. Shain fought to regain control, his every move a desperate dance between survival and annihilation. He rerouted power, sacrificing non-essential systems to keep the engines and shields marginally functional.

The chase took them through asteroid fields, the Starseeker weaving between jagged rocks, each near miss a testament to Shain's piloting skill. The Eradicators' ships, sleek and deadly, pursued them relentlessly, their movements precise and coordinated, hinting at a superior intelligence guiding their assault. They used the asteroids to their advantage, launching surprise attacks from unexpected angles.

Shain applied every trick he knew, using the Starseeker's agility to outmaneuver the larger, heavier Eradicator ships. He activated the ship's cloaking device, a risky move given its depleted power reserves, hoping to briefly escape the onslaught. The darkness of space swallowed them, offering a temporary respite from the relentless barrage. But the cloaking device was weak, flickering intermittently, its effectiveness compromised by the damage to the ship's systems.

The brief respite was shattered when a powerful energy pulse ripped through the cloaking field, momentarily blinding them. Shain cursed as the Starseeker's shields overloaded and collapsed, leaving them vulnerable. A hail of energy blasts pounded the hull, sending tremors through the ship.

"We need to lose them," Shain yelled over the roaring alarms. "There's a nebula ahead. The density should help us evade their sensors."

The nebula, a swirling mass of cosmic dust and gas, was a dangerous gamble. Navigation would be difficult, and the limited visibility would offer little protection from the Eradicators. But it was their only chance.

They plunged into the asteroid field, the Starseeker weaving through jagged debris. Shain's reflexes were a blur, threading the ship through lethal gaps. The Eradicators' pursuit continued, their ships attempting to track them through the chaos, their targeting systems struggling with the interference. The sensors on the Starseeker sputtered and crackled; the nebula was a battlefield of disoriented energy readings, static, and interference.

Shain worked on instinct, guided by Echo, relying on her sensitivity to cosmic vibrations to avoid collisions with large asteroids and maintain his course. The nebula was a chaotic labyrinth, a maelstrom of energy fluctuations, and the Eradicators, despite their advanced technology, struggled to maintain pursuit.

But their respite was short-lived. The Eradicators were persistent, employing advanced sensor technology that penetrated the nebula's interference to some extent. They sent out waves of energy to trace the Starseeker's location, keeping it from escaping. Shain had to constantly adapt his maneuvers, staying ahead of the incoming sensors.

Their desperate flight continued for what seemed like an eternity. The Starseeker's systems were failing alarmingly; power levels were critically low, and the ship's structural

integrity was compromised in several places. With each passing moment, their chances of survival diminished.

Then, through the swirling chaos of the nebula, Shain spotted a glimmer of hope—a small, uncharted system, shielded from the prying eyes of the galactic Council and the relentless pursuit of the Eradicators. It was a long shot, a slim chance of survival, but it was the best they had. He navigated the ship through the nebula towards the hidden system, guiding them towards this potentially life-saving sanctuary.

The Eradicators, their sensors still struggling, were losing track of the Starseeker in the nebula. Their relentless pursuit slowed, hampered by the chaotic conditions. Shain, using every ounce of his skill and ingenuity, managed to lead them astray, guiding the crippled Starseeker into the system's outer rim.

They emerged from the nebula into the relative calm of the hidden system, their escape both thrilling and precarious. The system was a forgotten corner of the galaxy, home to a sparse collection of ancient celestial bodies devoid of major planets and star systems. It was the perfect hiding place. The Starseeker, damaged but intact, limped into a hidden asteroid field, using the dense asteroid field as a shield and a hiding place.

The immediate danger had passed, but the threat of the Eradicators remained. Shain knew they wouldn't give up easily. They needed to repair the ship, reinforce their defenses, and continue their fight to amplify the song and restore balance to the cosmos. The chase had been a brutal and terrifying experience,

but it had bought them precious time; they had won it, nothing more.

The silence that followed their escape was filled with a new type of tension, the quiet hum of determination in the face of impending danger. The fight was far from over. It was the beginning of a larger struggle.

Shain's hands trembled as he stabilized the Starseeker, the ship's hum now a faint echo of the Iridian song. The revelations from prior chapters—Kaelis's betrayal, Veyra's shadow, Silentium's reach, the Pulse Shard, the Star Veil, the Resonance Binding, the Cosmic Weaving, the Eradicators' archive, the voices of the fallen, Echo's role as the last spark, Shain's resolve, the reality-manipulation engine, and their alliance—wove a tapestry of dread and purpose. His mind drifted to Sylara, a planet of harmonic mists where he'd arrested a poet, Lirien Vex, who'd sung of the Resonance Codex, a ritual that encoded the Iridian song into relics to preserve their cosmic connection. Sylara's mists were erased in a "solar flare," Lirien's verses buried. Now, her songs echoed in the nebula's pulse, urging him to act.

He approached Echo, her serene expression unshaken despite the ship's near-destruction. "The Codex," Shain said, his voice rough with exhaustion, "it guided us through the nebula. You felt the song, didn't you? How do we use it now?"

Echo's eyes gleamed, a mix of sorrow and defiance. "The Resonance Codex is our truth, Shain. It encoded our song into the cosmic web, into relics like the Resonance Key. I'm its conduit,

the last spark. The Key can amplify it, restore the song, but Veyra's vessel seeks to silence it through Silentium."

Shain's pulse quickened. The Resonance Key, the final relic, could undo the Eradicators' erasure. He recalled the Sylaran Rift's sentient pulse, amplifying the song's signal. Was the Key reaching out? He called Jax and Rix to the bridge, their faces etched with fatigue. "The Resonance Codex," Shain said, sharing Echo's words. "It's how the Iridians preserved their song. We need the Key, but the Eradicators are still out there."

Jax's eyes widened, his hand tightening on his rifle. "Sir, I felt it— the song. In the nebula, it was like it was guiding me, singing through the chaos. It's real, but it's heavy, pulling me somewhere."

Rix nodded, his voice tense. "The signal's spiking, sir. It's syncing with the rift, disrupting ORION's core. I found another subroutine—Silentium's code, rerouting our cloaking systems to an Eradicator beacon."

Shain's stomach twisted. He accessed the ship's archives, digging for references to the Resonance Codex. A redacted file surfaced, labeled "Veil Protocol: Silent Abyss," detailing a Council operation to suppress harmonic relics. Sylara, Voryn, Kryon—all targeted, all erased. The Resonance Key was listed as a "cosmic disruptor," capable of amplifying the song to shatter Silentium's control. Veyra was its hunter, her rogue status a cover for her Eradicator allegiance.

Shain shared the file with Echo. "The Key—it's in Valthara's rift, with the Silent Choir. But Veyra's vessel is still tracking us. How do we use the Codex to protect it?"

Echo's voice was a soft hum, resonating with the ship's pulse. "The Codex is our shield, Shain. It weaves us to the song, to each other. The Choir will guide us, but Silentium's agents are among you. Trust the song, but watch your crew."

Her words chilled him. Kaelis, Vorn, Lira, Vara, Taryn, Myra—how many more were compromised? He ordered Rix to scan the ship for Silentium's code, fearing another infiltrator. The scan revealed a micro-device in the sensor array, pulsing with Eradicator runes, broadcasting their position. "Another saboteur," Shain muttered, sprinting to the sensor bay with Jax.

There, Ensign Koren stood by the controls, her eyes glassy, a device in her hand. "Koren, stop!" Shain shouted, his pistol raised. Her voice was mechanical: "The Silence demands her." Jax tackled her, Shain disabling the device, but the sensors flickered, exposing their location. Alarms blared, the nebula's pulse surging outside, the air crackling with energy.

Echo's voice came through the comms, calm but urgent. "Sing, Shain. The Key's rhythm can shield us." Jax and Shain hummed, their voices unsteady but growing stronger, syncing with the rift's pulse. Echo joined, her harmony weaving through the ship, silencing the array. Koren collapsed, her eyes clearing. "Veyra… she's in the rift," she gasped.

Shain restrained Koren, his mind reeling. Silentium's implants were pervasive, Veyra's influence a shadow in their minds. He

returned to the bridge, where an alarm blared: "Vessel detected—Silentium signature." The sensors showed the obsidian Eradicator ship, its hull etched with runes, broadcasting Veyra's voice: "Surrender the Iridian, or the Key is ours."

Shain's hand hovered over the weapons console, but Echo's voice stopped him. "The song, Shain. It's our shield." Jax, Rix, and Echo sang, their harmony resonating through the ship, disrupting the vessel's systems. Shain joined, the vibration shaking his core, forcing the ship to retreat into the nebula's mists.

The crew's tension flared, whispers of mutiny resurfacing. Ensign Lira's voice echoed: "She's controlling us!" Shain silenced her, his voice firm. "The song's saving us, Lira. The Eradicators are the threat." He ordered neural scans, revealing no new implants, but the crew's fear of the song grew, a fracture he couldn't mend.

A new transmission arrived, untraceable, from the Silent Choir: "Starseeker, the Key sings in Valthara's rift. Encode it with the Codex, or Silentium consumes all." Shain shared it with Jax and Rix, their resolve strengthening. "We're in, sir," Jax said, his voice steady. "For the song."

The Starseeker limped into the hidden system, its systems barely functional. ORION's voice crackled: "Anomaly detected—rift core unstable." Shain pulled up the sensors, spotting a shimmering vortex in the nebula, its rhythm chaotic, corrupted by Silentium. Echo's voice guided them: "Sing through it, Shain. The Key's there."

Shain, Jax, and Rix sang, their voices weaving with Echo's, stabilizing the vortex. The Resonance Key's pulse emerged, a beacon to Valthara. Shain's heart pounded—he was no longer just a marshal, but a singer, carrying the Iridian song against a galaxy that sought to silence it.

The journey through the Sylaran Nebula remained perilous, the rift's sentient pulse amplifying the song's effects. Shain's memories surged—Lirien Vex's verses, Myra Vex's research, Vara Kess's studies—all pointing to the song's power. He sat with Echo, her calm anchoring him. "Tell me about the Resonance Codex," he said. "How does it restore the song?"

Echo's voice was a melody, weaving through the hum. "The Codex is a vow, Shain. Iridians encoded their essence into the relics, tying them to the cosmic web. The Key amplifies, the Stone remembers, the Shard guides, the Veil protects. Together, they can restore the song, awaken the galaxy. Valthara's choir awaits, but Veyra's vessel is closing in."

Shain's resolve hardened. He recalled Sylara's mists, their harmonic glow fading under Council fire. "Can we encode it? Here, now?"

Echo's smile was faint but resolute. "You're already encoding, Shain. You, Jax, Rix—you're part of the song. Trust it, and it'll guide us to Valthara."

The crew's unrest lingered, fear of the song spreading. Shain faced a dilemma: amplify the song through the ship's systems, risking Silentium's detection, or trust the Choir's guidance to

Valthara. He shared the choice with Echo. "Amplifying it could counter Veyra's vessel," he said. "But it might expose us."

Echo's eyes gleamed. "The song is our truth, Shain. Amplify it, but trust the Choir. They'll protect us."

Shain rerouted power to the comms array, amplifying the song's pulse. The Starseeker vibrated, the nebula's rift glowing brighter, but Veyra's vessel returned, its runes pulsing. Shain, Jax, Rix, and Echo sang, their harmony a shield, forcing the vessel to retreat. The Key's pulse grew, guiding them to Valthara, the song's truth their only hope.

Shain's memories of Sylara resurfaced—nights studying Lirien's verses, her warnings about the Eradicators' reach. The song echoed those warnings, a truth he'd buried under years of duty. On the bridge, the nebula's mists swirled, and Shain felt the song's presence—not just in Echo, but in himself, in Jax, in Rix, in the Starseeker's hum. The Eradicators sought to silence it, but Shain, the reluctant marshal, was now its conductor, determined to let the galaxy hear its melody.

Tactical Maneuvers

The asteroid field was a maze of jagged rock and drifting dust, a chaotic ballet of celestial bodies hurtling through the void. Shain, drawing on years of navigating the perilous lanes of uncharted space, guided the Starseeker with expert precision. Every turn was a gamble, every near-miss a whispered flirtation with death. He relied on his instinct honed and training of years dealing with space lanes. Every move was worth it. The ship groaned under the strain, its battered hull protesting with each near-miss collision. The Eradicators, however, were relentless, their pursuit ships weaving through the field with chilling precision, their movements eerily synchronized, as if guided by a single, malevolent mind.

Their advanced sensor technology, designed to pierce the dust clouds and detect the Starseeker's faint energy signature, constantly probed the field, sending a relentless barrage of probing energy pulses. Shain countered this with a series of audacious maneuvers, using the asteroids as both shields and weapons, employing a chaotic dance of evasive tactics honed through years of experience in the lawless sectors of space. He used the erratic gravitational pulls of the asteroids to slingshot the Starseeker around corners, forcing the pursuing vessels to

compensate for unexpected changes in trajectory. It was a desperate game of cat and mouse, played against the backdrop of a silent, unforgiving cosmos.

Echo, despite the ever-present threat, remained remarkably calm, as if it had braced itself for any upcoming alarming situation. Her connection to the cosmic vibrations allowed her to sense the subtle shifts in the gravitational field, providing Shain with vital information that allowed him to anticipate the movements of the Eradicators' ships. Her guidance became essential, an unseen hand guiding him through the treacherous field, preventing collisions and alerting him to unseen dangers lurking in the darkness between the asteroids. Occasionally, she would murmur cryptic warnings, her voice a low hum against the backdrop of the ship's strained mechanics, warning of impending energy bursts or hidden pursuers.

With no second thought, Shain activated the Starseeker's ancient, near-obsolete ECM – a relic from another era, barely operational and draining their already failing power reserves, a desperate gamble considering the ship's depleted power reserves. The old system, a relic from a bygone era of spacefaring, produced a barrage of electronic noise, a chaotic storm of confusing signals designed to jam the eradicators' advanced sensors and disrupt their targeting systems. It was a crude technique, but in this desperate situation, it was all they had. The ECM pulse momentarily blinded their pursuers, creating a brief window of opportunity.

Seizing the moment, Shain responded with a flurry of bold maneuvers, turning the chaos of the asteroid field to his

advantage. The task was full of maneuver was fraught with danger, pushing the ship's capabilities to their absolute limit, but it proved effective. The Eradicators' ships, caught off guard and disoriented by the ECM burst, momentarily lost track of the Starseeker in the chaos of the asteroid field. They were forced to slow their pursuit, cautiously navigating the dense field to avoid collisions. The chaos they sought to impose on Shain now slowed them significantly.

But the respite existed for a very brief period. The Eradicators were patient and persistent, their technology far exceeding the Starseeker's outdated systems. They utilized their superior technology wisely and wielded it with unrelenting focus. They strategically cleared a path through the asteroid field, their energy weapons vaporizing smaller rocks to create a clear trajectory, inching closer to their target. Their pursuit ships used brute force and subtle maneuvers, using the larger asteroids as cover while systematically eliminating smaller obstacles.

Shain, however, was not defeated. He knew that relying solely on evasion would ultimately lead to their demise. He needed a more strategic approach. He studied the Eradicators' tactics, observing their patterns, identifying their weaknesses. And Shain had connected the dots. He discovered they were too reliant on their superior technology, too dependent on precision, too confident in their relentless pursuit. And this is where they were mistaken.

Utilizing the Starseeker's limited maneuvering thrusters and Echo's guidance, Shain began to exploit the flaws in the Eradicators' strategy. He executed a series of unpredictable, seemingly erratic maneuvers, deliberately creating chaos and

confusion. He took advantage of unexpected gravitational shifts, using them to abruptly alter his course, leaving the Eradicators scrambling to keep up and maintain their precise targeting systems. He led them on a wild goose chase, using the density of the asteroid field as a shield. The unpredictability of his moves threw off the Eradicators' perfectly coordinated pursuit; their automated targeting systems, designed for precise, calculated attacks, struggled to keep pace with the chaotic dance Shain orchestrated. It was a desperate gambit, a fight for survival played out in the shadow of countless rocks hurtling through space.

He lured them deeper into the asteroid field, led them into a knot of dense rock and gravitational anomalies. The Eradicators followed – and paid the price. These anomalies, unpredictable pockets of strong gravitational forces, caused unexpected shifts in trajectory, making it extremely difficult to maintain a constant course. Shain used these areas to his advantage, exploiting the Eradicators' reliance on precise calculations and their inability to predict the unpredictable pulls of these gravitational forces accurately.

As the Eradicators' ships struggled to adapt, Shain seized the opportunity. He executed a series of sharp turns and rapid accelerations, utilizing the erratic gravitational forces to disorient and separate their pursuers. He led them into a region of the field where the asteroid density was at its highest, where even their advanced sensors struggled to penetrate the chaotic energy readings. It was a dangerous maneuver, risking collision, but it bought them precious time.

In the ensuing chaos, several of the Eradicators' pursuit ships collided with each other and with asteroids, causing a massive explosion in a fiery display of destruction. The resulting debris cloud further obscured the Starseeker's location, shielding them from the remaining pursuers. Using this chaos to his advantage, Shain guided the Starseeker through the debris field, expertly avoiding the hazardous wreckage. Emerging from the chaos, battered but still functioning, the Starseeker found itself momentarily free from immediate pursuit.

The Eradicators had been temporarily disoriented and scattered, their superior technology momentarily rendered useless by the chaos they sought to impose on Shain. They had survived, but the battle was far from over. The relentless pursuit would resume, and they had to be prepared. The silent, cold vacuum of space was a harsh mistress, and the chase was far from over. The pursuit ships, damaged and scattered, would regroup, and the hunt would continue. The escape was temporary, a brief respite before the next stage of the desperate fight for survival. The universe held its breath, vast and silent, watched and waited for their fate to unfold.

Echos Resistance

The quiet was deceptive—a fragile pause in the storm of their escape. The temporary reprieve was a fragile thing, a fleeting moment of calm in the maelstrom of their desperate flight. The silence of space, usually a suffocating emptiness, now felt strangely comforting, a stark contrast to the relentless hum of the Eradicators'pursuit ships that had been their constant companion for what felt like an eternity. Shain, his face etched with exhaustion, ran a hand through his already disheveled hair, his eyes scanning the sensor readings. The respite wouldn't last.

Echo, seated quietly in the observation deck, seemed to sense his apprehension. She didn't speak, but a subtle shift in her posture, a barely perceptible change in the rhythm of her breathing, betrayed a hidden intensity. Her eyes, usually pools of calm reflection, now held a spark of something else–something akin to defiance. Shain had assumed her quiet demeanor stemmed from resignation, a passive acceptance of her fate. He was wrong.

Suddenly, a low vibration rippled through the Starseeker, hum resonated through the Starseeker, a vibration that seemed to emanate from within the ship itself. It wasn't the groan of stressed metal, nor the whine of failing engines; different from

the usual groans of strained metal, it felt like a deeper and more resonant frequency. Shain's heart pounded in his chest. It was subtle, almost imperceptible to the untrained ear, but he recognized it. It was a manipulation of the ship's energy flow, a subtle adjustment that optimized the engines' performance, a slight realignment of the shields.

He glanced at Echo, his eyes widening in surprise. She was humming faintly, her eyes closed, her fingers tracing patterns in the air, almost as if she were conducting an orchestra of unseen forces. The hum intensified, and the Starseeker responded, its battered engines roaring back to life with renewed vigor, a surge of power coursing through its aging systems. The shields, previously flickering and weak, solidified, strengthening their energy signature.

Shain watched, awestruck. Echo wasn't just sensing the ship's vibrations. She was shaping them – adjusting the Starseeker's energy field as if it were an extension of herself, intuitive perception; this was control, a deliberate manipulation of the ship's systems using something far beyond standard technology. The cosmic vibrations she sensed weren't just passive observations; she was actively interacting with them, weaving them into the fabric of the ship's energy field. It was a display of power that bordered on the miraculous.

"You... you're manipulating the ship's energy," Shain stammered, his voice laced with a mixture of awe and disbelief.

Echo opened her eyes, her gaze steady and unwavering. "The vibrations are everywhere" she said, her voice a quiet hum,

"They resonate through everything. The ship, the asteroids, even the void between the stars. I can feel their flow, their patterns. And I can influence them."

Her words were a revelation and suddenly it all made sense – her intuition, her timing, the whispers of the lost Iridians. The whispers of the erased Iridians, the subtle changes in gravitational fields – everything began to make sense. Echo wasn't just a survivor; she was a conduit, a living link to a power that the Eradicators desperately sought to erase. Her connection to the cosmic vibrations was a weapon, a formidable force that challenged their superior technology.

But the respite was fleeting. The Eradicators' pursuit ships, regrouped and repaired, resumed their relentless advance. They were adapting, their attacks becoming more sophisticated and insidious with each move. They weren't merely pursuing; they were hunting, patiently tracking the Starseeker through the labyrinthine asteroid field, probing for weaknesses, and exploiting vulnerabilities.

Echo, however, was ready. She anticipated their attacks, sensing their movements before their ships even registered on the Starseeker's sensors. She used the cosmic vibrations to subtly alter the ship's trajectory, creating unexpected shifts in momentum, throwing off their targeting systems. She intensified the energy field around the Starseeker, creating localized disruptions that shielded them from their weapons.

The chase became a terrifying game of cosmic chess, a dance between sophisticated technology and an almost mystical ability.

Shain, operating the ship's controls with renewed purpose, found himself working in perfect harmony with Echo, their actions flawlessly synchronized. He provided the tactical maneuvering, while she controlled the underlying energies, forming a symbiotic partnership born from desperation and a shared determination to survive.

The Eradicators responded with escalating force. They deployed energy weapons capable of piercing the Starseeker's reinforced shields, their attacks increasingly precise and relentless. The ship shuddered under the barrage, its hull groaning under the relentless pounding. Shain fought to maintain control, his knuckles white as he gripped the controls, his heart pounding.

But Echo's abilities were evolving. As the battle intensified, her control over the cosmic vibrations grew stronger, more precise. She learned to amplify certain frequencies, creating localized gravitational disturbances that threw the Eradicators' ships off course, causing them to collide with each other and the asteroids. She harnessed the energy of the field, transforming it into a shield, a weapon, a tool to defend their fragile craft.

The battle raged on, a desperate struggle for survival played out amidst the chaotic beauty of the asteroid field. The Starseeker, battered but defiant, navigated the treacherous landscape, dodging energy blasts, weaving through fields of debris, relying on both Shain's skill and Echo's uncanny connection to the cosmos. The lines between science and mysticism blurred as they fought, a testament to their shared determination.

The chase stretched on for what felt like days, the relentless pursuit punctuated by moments of intense combat and fleeting periods of desperate evasion. Shain pushed the Starseeker to its limits, performing maneuvers that defied both logic and probability, guided by Echo's uncanny insights into the subtle currents of the cosmic vibrations.

As they plunged deeper into the field, they encountered regions of unusual gravitational anomalies. These pockets of warped spacetime was dangerous, capable of tearing a ship apart, but Echo's ability to sense and manipulate them gave them an unexpected advantage. She used them to disorient the Eradicators' ships, trapping them in unpredictable gravitational wells and creating chaos amongst their ranks.

The Eradicators, accustomed to precision and calculated attacks, struggled to adapt to this unpredictable environment. Their sophisticated targeting systems failed to function accurately in the face of constantly shifting gravitational fields. Their perfect coordination began to fracture, their relentless pursuit faltering amidst the chaos they themselves were inadvertently creating.

The Starseeker, battered but unbowed, used this disarray to its advantage, weaving through the gravitational anomalies, exploiting the weaknesses of the Eradicators' fleet. Shain, guided by Echo's insights, navigated through the most chaotic regions, forcing the Eradicators into ever more desperate situations.

With a final, daring dive, Shain plunged the Starseeker into a particularly dense cluster of asteroids, using the chaotic environment to mask their escape. The Eradicators, blinded by

the asteroid debris and disoriented by the gravitational anomalies, lost sight of the Starseeker. They were left in the chaos of their own making, their superior technology rendered useless in the face of the unpredictable power of the cosmos.

Emerging from the asteroid field, battered but alive, Shain and Echo found themselves free, at least for now. Together, they became undefeatable. Their pursuers were scattered, their coordination broken, their technology tested to its limits. They had cheated death, narrowly escaping the clutches of the relentless Eradicators. But even in this fleeting moment of victory, they knew that the chase was not over. The Eradicators were persistent, their motives still shrouded in mystery, their ultimate goal yet to be revealed. The fight for survival, for the truth, and the preservation of Echo wasn't a passenger. She was the resistance.

And the legacy of her people—the truth they died to protect— was no longer forgotten. It pulsed through her like a song waiting to be sung. Echo's people's legacy had only just begun, the battle has just begun with a long road to go. On their way to success, many things are to unravel, many mysteries, secrets and what not.

Unexpected Ally

The silence aboard the Starseeker was deafening in the wake of their perilous escape from the asteroid field, filled with the unspoken knowledge that their reprieve was temporary. The battered Starseeker, a testament to their desperate flight, hummed with a low thrum, a symphony of stressed metal and barely functioning systems.

Shain ran a hand over the scorched console, the heat still radiating from the overloaded engines. His bloodshot eyes drifted to Echo, who sat in quiet contemplation, almost motionless on the observation deck, her face serene despite the ordeal they had just endured.

The relief was palpable, yet a knot of unease tightened in Shain's gut. The Eradicators wouldn't simply vanish. Their resources were vast, their reach extensive, and their determination to erase Echo and everything she represented was unwavering. He knew this escape was merely a tactical retreat, a brief respite before the next, inevitable wave of attacks.

Suddenly, a flicker on the long-range sensor display caught his attention. It wasn't the telltale signature of an Eradicator

warship; this was different, fainter, more… subtle. A small, almost insignificant blip, nestled amongst the cosmic background noise. He zoomed in, his breath catching in his throat. The blip was a vessel, small and nimble, unlike anything he had encountered before. It was approaching the Starseeker, its trajectory converging with theirs.

"Echo," Shain whispered, his voice hoarse, "what do you make of this?"

Echo opened her eyes, her gaze fixed on the approaching vessel. She didn't speak for a long moment, her fingers tracing patterns in the midair as if feeling the subtle vibrations emanating from the approaching ship. Then, a faint smile touched her lips – a rare and unexpected expression that sent a jolt of surprise through Shain.

"It's… different," she finally said, her voice low and hesitant. "The vibrations… they aren't the same. There's… a dissonance. A discord within the usual harmonic resonance."

As the small ship drew closer, its identity remained a mystery, still making no aggressive move. As it aligned alongside the *Starseeker*, the comms crackled to life. threatening, unlike the aggressive tactics of the Eradicators. As it finally aligned itself beside the Starseeker, a message crackled through the comms system, its language surprisingly familiar, albeit laced with a heavy accent Shain couldn't place.

"This is… Khel," the voice static laced with tension. "I… I believe we share a common interest - in the survival of certain individuals."

Shain and Echo exchanged a look. Khel? The name echoed with a familiar ring, though the origin eluded them both. Intrigued and wary, Shain responded, his voice cautiously neutral. "Identify yourself. State your purpose."

"I am Khel," the voice repeated, gaining confidence. "A former agent of the Eradicators. I have information... crucial information regarding their plans, their weaknesses... I can help you."

The revelation hung in the air, it hit something in Shain's memory like a half-remembered dream. He and echo exchanged a wary glance. Suspicion writhed beneath his skin. A disillusioned Eradicator agent offering their assistance? It seemed too good to be true, a plot twist ripped from the pages of a cheap space opera. Yet, the desperation in Khel's voice, the genuine tremor in the faint static of the comms, felt real.

"Why?" Shain asked, suspicion coloring his voice. "Why should we trust you?"

"Because," Khel replied, "the Eradicators are not what you think they are. They claim to be preserving order, but they are destroying history, rewriting reality, wiping out entire civilizations for their own twisted ambitions. I... I witnessed it firsthand. I participated. I regret it deeply."

What unfolded next shattered every assumption they held. Khel's confession unravelled a tapestry of lies and deception. He revealed the Eradicators weren't a monolithic organization but a fractured group, divided by internal conflicts and rivalries. Their leader, a shadowy figure known only as the Architect, controlled

the flow of information, manipulating events to maintain his power and control. He manipulated the narrative of the Iridian extinction, twisting the truth to suit his agenda. The psychic plague, the metaphysical weapon – all fabrications to justify his actions and conceal his true motives.

Khel detailed the Eradicators' internal communications, their coded messages, their logistical weaknesses. He described their advanced technology, their surveillance network, their hidden bases scattered across the galaxy. The architect's true ambition, Khel revealed was godlike: the manipulation of cosmic vibration – an energy Echo herself had barely begun to master. It was a power similar to Echo's but far more destructive and less refined. The Architect sought to exploit these vibrations to rewrite history, erasing civilizations he deemed undesirable, reshaping the galaxy according to his own twisted vision.

He was close to something terrible. He revealed the existence of a hidden base, a subterranean fortress on a remote planet, where the Architect conducted his experiments. This base held the key to dismantling the Eradicators, potentially even undoing some of the irreversible damage they had caused. The location, however, was heavily guarded, surrounded by an impenetrable energy field, protected by advanced weaponry that would defy even the Starseeker's enhanced capabilities.

"Their technology is impressive," Khel admitted, "but it's not invulnerable. There are weak points, vulnerabilities... I can help you exploit them. But you must hurry. The Architect is aware of my defection. He's hunting me."

As the implications of Khel's revelations sunk in, the weight of their situation felt even heavier. The chase had escalated from a desperate flight for survival into a galaxy-spanning struggle against a far more significant and dangerous foe than they had initially imagined. This wasn't just about rescuing Echo; it was about preventing the complete rewriting of galactic history, the erasure of countless civilizations and the subjugation of free will itself.

Shain knew that trusting Khel was a gamble, a leap of faith into the unknown. But the alternative – continuing their desperate flight, evading the relentless pursuit of the Eradicators with no clear strategy, no real hope of victory – was even less appealing. He had nothing left to lose.

"Alright, Khel," Shain said, his voice firm despite the tremor in his hands. "Tell me what we need to do."

The reply came swiftly. Khel outlined a plan, his voice crackled through the comms, outlining a daring plan. It was a long shot, a suicide mission, a gamble against impossible odds. But, with the combined knowledge of Khel's inside information, Echo's uncanny ability to manipulate cosmic vibrations, and Shain's tactical brilliance, it was their only chance.

The chase resumed – but now with purpose. The starseeker wasn't just fleeing anymore. It was hunting, strategizing. Fighting not just for survival, but for the soul of the galaxy. Khel's appearance had changed everything. The unexpected ally had shifted the odds, adding a crucial layer of complexity and hope to their struggle. But the risk remained: Khel could be wrong, the

plan might fail, and their enemy, far from defeated, was stronger and more cunning than they had ever imagined. The stakes had never been higher. The fight for the galaxy's future had truly begun.

Desperate Measures

The Starseeker groaned in protest, producing a cacophony of protesting metal and strained machinery. Its battered frame trembling with every labored pulse of its failing systems, the warning lights blinked a frantic rhythm across the console, each flash a stark reminder of their precarious situation. The engines sputtered, threatening to fail entirely, leaving them adrift in the unforgiving expanse of space, a sitting duck for the Eradicators' relentless pursuit. Their escape from the asteroid field had been miraculous, a stroke of luck amidst a maelstrom of chaos, but the reprieve was fleeting.

Shain wrestled with the controls, his knuckles white against the worn metal. He'd patched the damaged systems together with makeshift repairs, jury-rigging the Starseeker's failing life support, navigation, and propulsion systems. Each maneuver felt like walking a tightrope, one misstep away from a catastrophic failure. The ship was limping, bleeding energy with every strained thrust of its battered engines, each second inching them closer to oblivion.

Echo, ever stoic, stood nearby, observed the frantic activity with a disconcerting calm. It felt like an unsettling pillar of calm had

settled upon her amid this relentless chaos. Her eyes, reflecting the flickering lights, held a depth of understanding that both unsettled and reassured Shain. She seemed to sense the delicate balance, the precariousness of their situation, as acutely as he did, yet she remained unnervingly composed.

"We can't outrun them," Shain muttered, his voice tight with stress, his gaze fixed on the sensor readings. "They'll catch us eventually."

Echo's gaze drifted to the viewport, where the cold, unforgiving blackness of space stretched towards the far reaches of the galaxy. The faintest shimmer of distant stars provided a weak and distant consolation.

"There's another way," she said, her voice barely a whisper, carrying a hint of something otherworldly. The words hung in the air, a promise and a threat intertwined.

Shain stared at her, skepticism warring with desperation. "Another way? What do you mean?"

Echo closed her eyes, her face serene, her fingers tracing patterns in the air, a silent dance with unseen forces. "The cosmic vibrations...I can use them. To... to mask our presence, to bend the very fabric of space-time around us." Her voice grew stronger, more confident with each word, laced with an otherworldly certainty.

"It's risky, Shain. Exceedingly risky. But it's our only chance."

The risk involved was immense. Manipulating the fabric of spacetime was far beyond anything Shain had ever encountered. It was a concept confined to theoretical physics, to esoteric discussions among the most brilliant minds in the galaxy, not a practical solution for escaping a deadly pursuit. It bordered on the mystical, on the impossible. Yet, the desperation of their situation left him with few other options. The alternative was certain death.

"How?" he asked, his voice strained, his hope clinging to a slender thread.

Echo's explanation was both precise and poetic. Her words spoke of resonance, harmonics, the alignment of the ship's energy signature with the rhythm of the cosmos. She spoke of manipulating resonant frequencies, by syncing with the natural vibrations of spacetime, creating a temporary distortion, a kind of "blind spot" that would conceal them from the Eradicators' advanced sensors, it would work as a pocket of nothing that would elude even the most sophisticated Eradicator tech. The process was delicate, requiring a precise understanding of cosmic vibrations and a level of control that seemed far beyond human comprehension.

The procedure began. Echo guided Shain, her instructions a blend of precise coordinates and intuitive adjustments. She directed him to reroute power, adjust the ship's shields, and fine-tune the engines to specific frequencies. The process was harrowing, the strain on the ship immense. Alarms blared, systems overloaded, and the Starseeker shuddered under the

stress. Shain fought to maintain control, sweat beading on his forehead, his heart pounding in his chest.

The ship groaned under the intense strain. The lights flickered, threatening to extinguish altogether, plunging them into darkness. The air thinned, the life support struggling to keep up. Every second

felt like an eternity, each adjustment a gamble with their very existence.

Then, a profound stillness enveloped the ship. The alarms ceased, the flickering lights stabilized, the engine's roar quieted to a low, almost reverent hum. The cacophony was soon replaced by an unannounced silence. The sensor reading blinked out. The Eradicators' pursuit vanished from their scans. They were gone.

It was as if they had vanished, not from space, but from reality itself. The Starseeker felt lighter, adrift, and disconnected from the cosmos, floating in a pocket of distorted spacetime.

The success of their desperate measure was profound. It was a testament to Echo's abilities, a breathtaking display of her connection to the cosmic web, and a horrifying glimpse into the raw power she wielded.

The silence, however, held an uneasy tranquility. They were safe, for now, but their escape was only temporary. Their desperate gambit had bought them time—but not safety. The Eradicators, with their immense resources and relentless determination, would eventually discover their deception. And the cosmic distortion, Echo warned, wouldn't last forever. The respite was a

brief reprieve, a pause before the next wave of the relentless chase. The true test was yet to come. The escape was a desperate gamble that had paid off, but the stakes remained as high as ever. The chase was far from over. The galaxy's fate teetered on the edge of a knife, on the shoulders of a runaway marshal and the last survivor of a vanished civilization.

The storm wasn't over.

The Unveiling

The silence of the warped spacetime was a heavy shroud – suffocating, yet oddly consoling. The Starseeker, adrift in its pocket of reality, felt strangely disconnected from the relentless pursuit that had driven them to this desperate measure. Echo, her face pale but resolute, leaned against the console, her breathing slow and even. The strain of manipulating spacetime had visibly depleted her, leaving her looking almost translucent.

Shain watched her, a tangle of awe and concern. He had witnessed the impossible – something that defied every physical law he understood. But the sense of relief was fleeting. This sanctuary was no more than a fragile bubble, soon to burst. Their escape was merely a tactical retreat, a postponement of the inevitable confrontation.

"Where to now?" Shain asked, his voice hoarse, the words catching in his throat.

Echo opened her eyes, their depths holding a vast, unsettling knowledge. "There's a place," she whispered, her voice weak but unwavering. "An abandoned station. A relic from a forgotten age. It holds... clues."

She projected a series of coordinates onto the screen, ghostly glimmers dancing across the dark console. The station, according to the scant information Echo managed to glean from the cosmic vibrations, was a clandestine research outpost, lost somewhere in the outer reaches of the Orion Arm. A place where secrets lay buried, waiting to be unearthed.

The journey was long and arduous. The Starseeker, its systems battered and worn, limped through the stellar abyss. Engines sputtered. Life supported flickered, the star-strewn canvas of space, its engines sputtering, its life support systems barely functioning. The silence was broken only by the rhythmic hum of the failing engines and the occasional crackle of static from the comms system.

Days bled into nights, though time itself felt meaningless. The endless expanse of space, punctuated only by the distant gleam of stars, pressed in on them, amplifying the sense of isolation and vulnerability. Shain fought to maintain the ship's integrity, patching holes, rerouting power, and constantly battling against the encroaching darkness.

Echo, weakened but unyielding, spent hours studying the faint whispers of the cosmic vibrations, piecing together fragments of information, unraveling the intricate tapestry of the galaxy's hidden history. She spoke of ancient civilizations, of forgotten technologies, of a cosmic consciousness that permeated all things. Her words hovered with a blend of science and mysticism, defying easy categorization, pushing the boundaries of Shain's understanding of reality.

Finally, after what felt like an eternity, the sensors detected a faint signal, a ghostly echo from a distant object. The abandoned space station, shrouded in an almost ethereal silence, appeared on the scanners, a skeletal silhouette against the vast backdrop of the cosmos.

The station emerged from the void, silhouetted against the distant stars. Its metallic structure was pitted and scarred, its once gleaming surfaces dulled and tarnished by the ravages of time and space. Dust motes danced in the faint light filtering through the shattered viewport, creating an eerie, almost mystical atmosphere.

Inside, the decay was even more profound. Derelict machinery lay scattered about, its wires tangled like the limbs of fallen giants. Dust covered everything, a thick layer concealing the station's secrets beneath a shroud of silence.

As Echo moved with an uncanny grace through the decaying corridors, her movements fluid and purposeful. She seemed to sense the hidden pathways, the forgotten chambers, her intuition guiding her through the labyrinthine structure. Shain followed, his every step echoing in the cavernous spaces, the silence punctuated only by his own labored breath.

They found a central chamber, a vast, circular room at the heart of the station. In the center of the room stood a single console, its surface surprisingly intact, its screen displaying a cryptic sequence of symbols and data streams.

As Echo touched the console, a wave of information washed over her, a torrent of data flooding her senses. She swayed, her face

paling, her breathing becoming ragged. The cosmic vibrations, it seemed, were stronger here, more potent, their whispers louder, more insistent.

When she finally regained her composure, her eyes were wide, filled with a profound understanding. She turned to Shain, her voice trembling slightly.

"The Eradicators... they aren't just eliminating civilizations," she said, her voice barely above a whisper. "They're rewriting history.

They're silencing any civilization that grasps the true interconnectedness of life, the cosmic resonance, the understanding of the universe as a living entity. They fear the power of a unified consciousness, the collective understanding of the cosmic vibrations. They want to maintain control, to keep the galaxy fragmented, isolated, vulnerable."

The data on the console revealed a chilling picture: the Eradicators were more than genocidal – they were editors of reality, rewriting galactic history to fit their own narrative, eliminating any trace of civilizations capable of transcending their limited understanding of reality. They were manipulating the very fabric of spacetime, altering records, suppressing information, and leaving no evidence of their actions.

The implications were shocking. Whatever they believed in, including the history books, the galactic archives, was potentially a lie, a carefully constructed illusion designed to maintain the Eradicators' control.

"They're afraid," Echo continued, her voice becoming strong, "of a unified consciousness, a galactic harmony based on understanding the cosmic resonance. A galaxy where the whispers of the universe are not only heard but understood. A galaxy that refuses to be controlled."

The abandoned station wasn't just a relic; it was a hidden archive, a repository of suppressed knowledge, a testament to the Eradicators'relentless campaign to control the galaxy. The discovery was a turning point, a revelation that shattered their previous understanding of the conflict and laid bare the Eradicators' true, terrifying ambition. The fight was no longer about rescuing a single civilization; it was about the future of the galaxy itself, the preservation of truth against a relentless tide of manipulation and control. The stakes had risen exponentially. Their escape had only bought them time; the real battle was just beginning. The galaxy's fate hung in the balance, resting on their ability to expose the Eradicators' machinations and awaken the galaxy to the truth. The fight for the soul of the galaxy had begun.

The Weapon

The console emitted a low hum, a thrumming vibration sound that resonated through the floor and into Shain's bones. What had once been an indecipherable tangle of symbols now resolved themselves into a coherent, if terrifying, narrative. Echo, her eyes closed, seemed to be absorbing the information directly, a conduit for the station's hidden knowledge. The air crackled with unseen energy, a palpable sense of revelation hanging heavy in the air.

When she finally opened her eyes, they glowed with a strange light - shone with an unsettling light, a mixture of horror and understanding. The pale cast of her skin had deepened, her face drawn and etched with the weight of the knowledge she now possessed. She didn't speak for a long moment, her gaze fixed on some distant point, her breath coming in ragged gasps. Shain watched, his heart pounding in his chest, a knot of dread tightening in his stomach. He knew, instinctively, that what she was about to reveal would change everything.

"It's not a plague," she finally whispered, her voice barely audible above the hum of the console. "Not in the traditional sense. It's... a disruption. A targeted disruption of the cosmic vibrations."

Shain frowned. "Cosmic vibrations? You mean... the song?"

Echo nodded, her movements slow and deliberate. "The song is the breath of the universe. It's the resonance – between minds, between worlds, between the living and the stars. It binds us, shapes us, defines our place in the grand weave. The Eradicators haven't destroyed civilizations by physical means; they've silenced them. They're cutting them off from the song."

She gestured to the console, her finger tracing the sequence of symbols now displayed clearly on the screen. "This technology...it's a weapon of silence. It doesn't kill; it erases. It disrupts the vibrational patterns, creating a localized void in the cosmic
resonance. The civilization affected ceases to exist, not just in physical reality, but in the collective consciousness. Their memory, their history, their very essence—it's as if they were never there."

Shain struggled to comprehend. A weapon that didn't destroy, but unwrote. Not death by force, but obliteration by forgetting. It was a weapon of unimaginable power, a technology that transcended conventional warfare. It wasn't about bombs or lasers or radiation; it was about the very fabric of reality itself. It was a weapon that eradicated not just bodies, but memories, erasing entire civilizations from the tapestry of existence.

"How... how is that possible?" Shain stammered, his mind reeling from the implications.

"Think of it like this," Echo explained patiently, sensing his confusion. "Every living thing, every star, every galaxy emits a

vibrational frequency. These frequencies intertwine, creating a symphony of existence, the cosmic song. The Eradicators' weapon disrupts this symphony. It targets specific frequencies, silencing individual civilizations, isolating them from the collective

consciousness. They are effectively deleted from the universe's memory."

"So, the Iridians... their song simply stopped?" Shain asked, his face paled and the pieces of the puzzle finally clicking into place.

"Yes," Echo confirmed, her voice filled with a profound sadness. "Their frequency was severed. The weapon didn't kill them outright; it silenced them, removed them from the cosmic tapestry. Their physical bodies may have perished, but their essence, their memory, their very existence was erased from the universal consciousness.

They're... gone."

The silence in the chamber was heavy, broken only by the faint hum of the console. The eradicators weren't just conquerors. They were editors of existence, rewriters of the cosmic script. He had stumbled upon a truth so vast, so terrifying, that it threatened to shatter his understanding of reality. The Eradicators weren't just conquerors; they were cosmic editors, rewriting the universe's narrative, manipulating its very fabric.

"But why?" Shain finally asked, his voice hoarse. "Why would they do this?"

Echo's gaze drifted to a fractured viewport, beyond which the stars burned in eternal silence "Control," she replied, her voice barely a whisper. "They fear the unity. They fear a galaxy connected by the song- aware, awake, beyond manipulation, field consciousness, the collective understanding of the cosmic vibrations. They fear the potential power of a galaxy united, a galaxy aware of its interconnectedness, a galaxy beyond their control. By silencing individual civilizations, by erasing their memory, they fragment the cosmos, preventing any unified consciousness from emerging."

The console pulsed again, displaying a new sequence of data and diagrams, a schematic of the weapon itself. It was an intricate device, a complex network of interwoven technologies, defying any simplistic explanation. It was a weapon not of brute force, but of subtle manipulation, a technology that worked on the very level of existence itself.

Shain examined the schematic, his mind racing to comprehend the implications, a chilling understanding unfolding in his mind. The weapon didn't destroy physical object in the traditional sense; it was a network, a distributed system capable of reaching across vast distances, targeting specific vibrational frequencies with terrifying precision. It was a weapon designed not to destroy, but to erase. To silence. To control.

The Eradicators' strategy became chillingly clear. They weren't interested in conquering planets or enslaving populations; their goal was far more insidious. They were manipulating the very fabric of reality, ensuring that certain civilizations – those who demonstrated an understanding of the cosmic vibrations, those

who possessed the potential to unite the galaxy – were systematically erased from existence, leaving no trace behind. Their weapon wasn't simply a tool of war; it was an instrument of historical revisionism, a technology designed to maintain their control over the galaxy by rewriting its past, present, and future.

The data on the console also revealed something else – the extent of their reach. The Eradicators' weapon was not a single device, but a network of subtly placed transmitters, strategically scattered throughout the galaxy, capable of simultaneously targeting multiple civilizations. The scale of their operation was staggering, an unimaginable conspiracy reaching across millennia, leaving no trace of its existence, except for the whispers of the silenced.

Echo leaned closer to the console, her fingers tracing the intricate patterns on the screen. She was piecing together more fragments of information, interpreting the complex data streams, unraveling the mysteries of the Eradicators' technology. She spoke of countermeasures, of ways to disrupt their signal, to restore the cosmic resonance, to awaken the galaxy to the truth.

But Shain could see the truth in her eyes, even as Echo spoke of hope, that the task ahead was monumental. The Eradicators had been operating in the shadows for eons, their power vast and their reach immeasurable. They were masters of manipulation, their control over information absolute. The fight to expose them, to awaken the galaxy to their treachery, would be the greatest battle of their lives. The fate of the galaxy rested on their shoulders, a burden of unimaginable weight. The silence of the erased echoed in the vastness of space, a chilling reminder of the

stakes. The weapon of silence was powerful, but so was the will to resist, the desire for truth, the yearning for connection in a galaxy desperately trying to remain whole.

The Confrontation

The airlock hissed, a metallic shriek that sliced through the suffocating silence of the corridor. Shain, his hand resting on the pulse rifle strapped to his thigh, felt a tremor of anticipation ripple through him, a mixture of fear and grim determination. Echo, her face pale but resolute, stood beside him, her eyes fixed on the darkened doorway ahead. They were at the heart of the Eradicator's stronghold, a labyrinthine structure carved into the very fabric of a derelict space station, a silent testament to the organization's insidious reach. The whispers of the silenced, the faint resonance of erased civilizations, hung heavy in the air, a constant, unsettling reminder of the stakes.

The doorway parted. A vast chamber bathed in an unsettling, ethereal glow. In the center, suspended in mid-air, was a platform of polished obsidian, upon which sat a figure – the leader of the Eradicators. The figure was humanoid in form, but its features were indistinct, blurred, as if viewed through a shimmering heat haze. Its movements were slow, deliberate, almost mechanical, devoid of any discernible emotion. There was no warmth in its gaze, no flicker of empathy in its eyes – only a

cold, calculating intelligence, a chilling emptiness that spoke volumes about the nature of its existence.

Shain raised his weapon, his finger resting lightly on the trigger. Echo remained silent, her eyes fixed on the figure, a strange mixture of fascination and revulsion reflected in their depths. The silence in the chamber was deafening, broken only by the faint hum of the Eradicators' technology, a low, throbbing resonance that seemed to penetrate their very bones.

The figure finally spoke, its voice a synthesized monotone, devoid of inflection or emotion. "You have come a long way, Marshal Combe. I commend your tenacity, your... persistence. But your efforts are futile. You cannot stop us." it echoed with a stripped tone.

Shain's grip tightened on the pulse rifle. "You call this control? This genocide? You've erased entire cultures, silenced entire species, all in the name of what – order? You call the eradication of entire civilizations order? You've silenced countless voices, erased millennia of history, all in the name of what? Some twisted notion of stability?"

the figure replied without a pause, its gaze unwavering. "Stability is essential. The universe is a chaotic place, Marshal Combe. Sentient life, in its unbridled expression, is a destabilizing force. We simply provide order, a framework within which the universe can function without collapsing into itself."

"And you achieve this order by silencing those who dissent?" Echo's voice, though soft, carried a surprising weight, a strength that belied her frail appearance. "By erasing memories,

obliterating civilizations, rewriting history? Is this the 'order' you envision? A sterile, empty universe, devoid of life, devoid of meaning?"

"Meaning is an illusion, a construct of the limited human mind," the figure responded, its tone unchanged. "Only order is real. Only control can guarantee survival."

Shain felt a surge of anger, a hot, white rage that threatened to consume him. "You think you're gods, manipulating the very fabric of existence? But you're nothing but parasites, feeding on the essence of life, twisting reality to serve your own twisted agenda."

"Our agenda, is nothing but, the preservation of the cosmos. Your emotional attachments, your sentimental notions of individual worth – these are weaknesses that lead to destruction. We have removed these weaknesses, we have purged the universe of its flaws, ensuring its continued existence." The figure rectified.

"And you call that preservation?" Echo challenged, her voice rising slightly. "It's genocide! You're not saving the universe; you're sterilizing it, leaving behind a desolate wasteland of erased memories and silenced voices. You claim order, but you've created nothing but emptiness."

The figure remained impassive, its face devoid of any expression. "Your arguments are emotionally driven, Marshal Combe. Your beliefs are based on subjective perceptions. You fail to grasp the grand design, the intricate workings of our plan. You cannot

understand the need for control, for order, for the eradication of chaos."

"I understand the need for compassion, for understanding, for empathy!" Shain shouted, his voice raw with emotion. "We may be frail, we may be flawed, but our imperfections are what make us human, what make us alive. Your perfect, sterile order is nothing more than a prison, a tomb for the universe."

The figure shifted slightly on its obsidian platform. "Your defiance is admirable, Marshal Combe, in a perverse sort of way. But it's
meaningless. Our technology is far beyond your comprehension. Our reach is infinite. We will continue to eradicate the destabilizing elements, the sources of chaos. You cannot stop us."

The figure raised a hand, and the chamber filled with a pulsating, ethereal light. The walls seemed to shimmer, the air crackled with unseen energy, and Shain felt a wave of nausea wash over him, a sense of disorientation, a feeling of being untethered from reality.

Echo, however, stood firm, her eyes blazing with defiance. "You may have the power to erase memories, to silence voices," she said, her voice firm and her resolute strong, "but you cannot erase the truth. You cannot silence the yearning for connection, the desire for understanding, the will to resist. We will fight you, and we will win."

The confrontation escalated, not with laser fire or explosions, but with a clash of wills, a battle between order and chaos, between control and freedom, between a chilling vision of a sterile,

controlled universe and the chaotic, vibrant tapestry of life in all its messy, beautiful imperfections. The fate of the galaxy hung precariously in the balance, the outcome of this clash determining not just the survival of Echo and Shain, but the very essence of existence itself. The fight for the soul of the universe had begun.

The whispers of the erased, once faint, now felt echoing with renewed strength, a silent chorus of defiance against the Eradicators and their cold, empty vision of a perfect, silent universe. The future remained uncertain, a battleground where hope and despair clashed, where the song of existence fought against the deafening silence of oblivion.

The Choice

The chamber pulsed with energy, an unseen pressure pressing against Shain's chest, distorting the air and space around him. The light intensified into something almost sentient, wrapping around them like a suffocating shroud. He felt a dizzying sense of vertigo, as if the very foundations of reality were shifting beneath his feet. The air crackled with unseen energy, a palpable tension that vibrated in his bones. Echo, however, remained unmoved, her eyes fixed on the Eradicator leader with a steely gaze that mirrored the unwavering strength of her convictions.

The leader's voice, that synthesized monotone, cut through the swirling energy. "The choice is yours, Marshal Combe. Destroy our central nexus, and risk unraveling the fabric of reality itself. The consequences are incalculable, the potential for universal collapse...immeasurable. Or, allow us to continue our work, to maintain the delicate balance, the essential order that prevents the universe from descending into chaos."

Shain's breath caught, he felt a cold dread creep into his heart. The choice was agonizing, a cruel dichotomy that presented no easy answers. One option offered the potential for salvation, but at the catastrophic cost of universal annihilation. The other

guaranteed the continuation of the Eradicators' reign of terror, a future where countless voices would remain silenced, countless civilizations erased from the tapestry of existence.

He turned to Echo, searching her face for any clue, any sign of guidance in this impossible dilemma. Her expression was unreadable, a mask of stoicism that hid the turmoil raging within. Yet, in the depths of her eyes, Shain saw a flicker of something else– a deep, unwavering resolve, a certainty that transcended the immediate threat, a conviction that ran deeper than the fear of annihilation.

"What happens if we destroy the nexus?" Shain asked, his voice barely a whisper against the pulsating energy of the chamber.

The Eradicator leader responded with the same chilling calmness. "The cosmic web, Marshal Combe, the threads that bind time, space, and being – would be severed," the Eradicator answered interconnectedness of all things, would be severed. The vibrations that bind the universe together would be disrupted. The consequences... are beyond human compre-hension. Imagine the universe as a finely tuned instrument. We are the caretakers, maintaining its delicate harmony. Destroy the nexus, and the instrument shatters."

Echo spoke, her voice soft but firm. "But isn't the universe already shattered? Isn't it already broken by your actions? By your silencing of voices, your erasure of civilizations? You speak of harmony, but your 'harmony' is built on the ashes of countless worlds, on the silenced cries of the erased."

"Order requires sacrifice," the Eradicator replied. "The few must suffer for the many. Individual lives are insignificant compared to the survival of the cosmos. Emotion clouds your judgment, Marshal Combe. You fail to grasp the grand design, the intricate workings of our plan. Your sentimental notions of life are irrelevant."

Shain's mind raced, trying to reconcile the two impossible choices. He imagined a universe plunged into chaos, a cosmic implosion that would erase all existence. Then he pictured the bleak alternative: a universe under the Eradicators' tyrannical control, a sterile, emotionless landscape devoid of life, a silent testament to their chilling vision of order.

The weight of the galaxy rested on his shoulders, the fate of countless civilizations hanging in the balance. He felt the crushing burden of responsibility, the agony of choosing between two equally terrifying outcomes. Each choice felt like a betrayal, a condemnation of the very essence of what it meant to be human, to be alive.

He looked again at Echo, searching her eyes for a sign, a glimmer of hope in this abyss of despair. He saw something beyond fear and hesitation, it was a quiet determination, a profound understanding of the stakes. She understood the magnitude of the choice, the potential consequences, yet her resolve remained unshaken.

"We can't let them win," she said, her voice barely above a whisper.

"We can't let them silence the universe. Even if it means risking everything."

A surge of energy erupted – not chaos, not destruction, but something else. Something deeper. The chamber trembled, and a great silence fell. The platform was empty. The eradicator leader was gone. The potential for catastrophic failure was overwhelming. But the alternative– surrender to the Eradicators, to their cold, empty vision of order –was unthinkable.

"Then we destroy the nexus," Shain said, his voice filled with a newfound resolve. "We risk everything, but we fight for the chance to preserve something more valuable than mere existence. We fight for the right to live, to feel, to connect, to exist as flawed, imperfect beings. We fight for the universe's soul."

The Eradicator leader remained impassive, its synthesized voice calm and devoid of emotion. "You have made your choice, Marshal Combe. Prepare for the consequences. The unraveling of the cosmic web will be... spectacular."

Shain raised his weapon, not at the Eradicator leader, but at the central nexus, a pulsating orb of energy that hummed with the power to unravel the very fabric of existence. He closed his eyes, bracing himself for the consequences, for the potential destruction of the universe itself.

But, as he fired, a wave of energy surged forth, not the expected destructive force, but something else entirely. The chamber shimmered, the air crackled, and then, silence. A profound,

unnerving silence, broken only by the faintest hum, a resonance that seemed to emanate from the depths of space itself.

When Shain opened his eyes, the obsidian platform was empty, the Eradicator leader vanished. The ethereal glow had faded, replaced by the cold, harsh light of the derelict space station. The humming persisted, a low, persistent thrum that resonated deep within their bones. They had destroyed the nexus, but instead of chaos, a strange new stillness had settled over the chamber, a quietude that hinted at something profoundly changed, something fundamentally altered within the fabric of reality. The whispers of the erased, once faint and fleeting, now resonated with a newfound clarity, a strength that spoke of resilience, of a universe that refused to be silenced.

The fight was far from over. The Eradicators might be gone, but the consequences of their actions, of their attempts to control and rewrite the universe, would ripple through existence for eons to come. The choice they made, the gamble they took, had altered the very nature of reality, creating a new, uncertain future where the balance between order and chaos, between control and freedom, remained precarious and ever-shifting. A new equilibrium would take time. It would be imperfect, messy, unpredictable. But it would be real. The universe, stripped of the Eradicators' artificial order, was now free to find its own equilibrium, a balance that would inevitably be chaotic, vibrant, and full of life in all its imperfect glory. The song of existence, once nearly silenced, now resonated with a renewed strength, a testament to the enduring power of hope, connection, and the will to resist. Shain and Echo, survivors of a cosmic war fought not with weapons, but with wills, stood at the precipice of a new

era, an era shaped by their choices and the reverberations of their actions echoing through the heart of the cosmos. The journey had just begun with something chilling to unfold.

A Gamble of Fate

The humming intensified – no longer a background murmur but a resonant, pulsing thrum that vibrated through the floor, coursing up through Shain's legs, and resonated deep within his chest cavity. It wasn't a sound of destruction, but of transformation – deep, undeniable, and almost unnerving. In the wake of the nexus's collapse, the silence that followed the destruction of the nexus was not one of absence. It vibrated with potential, brimming with a kind of energy that felt both alien and intimately familiar, a tangible shift in the very fabric of reality. The air itself seemed to hum with a newly awakened vitality.

Echo stood quietly beside him, her complexion pale, yet her eyes glowed with an eerie, radiant light. She reached out a hand, her fingers brushing against the smooth surface of the obsidian platform where the nexus had once pulsed with malevolent energy. Now, only a faint, shimmering residue remained, like heat rising from freshly cooled lava.

"It's... different," she whispered, her voice barely audible above the humming. "The vibrations... they're free."

A tide of exhaustion washed over him, the tension of the past hours finally releasing its grip. The weight of the galaxy, the burden of his decision, seemed to lift, replaced by a profound sense of... relief? Was it relief, or something more profound? A sense of liberation? He wasn't sure.

The space station, once a prison, now felt strangely empty, devoid of the oppressive atmosphere of the Eradicators. The silence was broken only by the rhythmic hum, a constant, low-level pulse that seemed to emanate from the very heart of the cosmos. It was a sound of change, a symphony of the universe re-tuning itself, shaking off the shackles of control.

Suddenly, a flicker of movement caught Shain's eye. A faint shimmer at the edge of his vision, like a heat haze rising from the metallic floor. He focused, squinting, and saw it again – a ripple in the air, a distortion of reality itself. The whispers of the erased Iridians, once faint and fragmented, were coalescing, forming a tangible presence.

One after another, the figures emerged from the shimmering fold in reality. They were translucent, ephemeral, caught in their forms flickering like candle flames in a draft, but their presence was undeniable. Their faces were etched with sorrow, but also with a quiet resilience, a strength born of their ordeal, a defiance that echoed in the steady hum that filled the chamber.

They were not ghosts. They were memory incarnate – presence reclaimed from the fringes of oblivion. Not extinguished. Their existence, previously confined to the fringes of reality, had been liberated by the destruction of the nexus. The artificial order

imposed by the Eradicators had been shattered, and the universe was revealing its true, multifaceted nature.

Shain watched in awe and wonder as the Iridians gathered, their ethereal forms coalescing into a shimmering cloud of light. They did not speak in words, but their collective consciousness resonated with an overwhelming sense of loss, of pain, but also of hope, of a future freed from the suffocating grip of the Eradicators' control.

The chamber was thick with energy – alive, electric, heavy with feeling. It felt like breathing in starlight,, thick and vibrant, a symphony of grief and hope intertwined. Shain felt a strange connection to these ethereal beings, a shared understanding of loss and resilience. He understood their pain, their longing for recognition, their desire to be remembered.

Echo stepped forward, her hand outstretched towards the shimmering cloud of Iridian forms. She closed her eyes, and a low, melodic hum escaped her lips, a song of remembrance, of compassion, of healing. The humming resonated with the pulse of the universe, weaving a tapestry of sound and energy that enveloped Shain and the ethereal figures.

The song flowed, it was not just music – it was a wave of pure empathy, washing over the chamber and resonating within Shain's soul. It was a song of sorrow, but also of strength, of hope and resilience. It spoke of the interconnectedness of all life, of the enduring power of the human spirit, of the resilience of the universe in the face of oppression. It was a song that spoke of the

power of memory, of the importance of remembering, of never letting the voices of the erased be silenced.

The song ended, and the ethereal forms of the Iridians began to fade, their light dissolving back into the shimmering distortion from whence they came. But as they faded, Shain felt a profound sense of connection, a shared understanding of loss and resilience, a sense of belonging to something larger than himself, larger than humanity.

He turned to Echo, and their eyes met. They shared a look of understanding, and in that silent exchange was everything – grief, triumph, understanding. The gamble they had taken, the risk they had embraced, had paid off. The universe was free, or at least, on its way to freedom.

The hum persisted, no longer a harbinger of dread but a constant reminder of the change that had occurred, a testament to the resilience of life, of memory, of the universe's refusal to be silenced. They had destroyed the nexus, but in doing so, they had unleashed a wave of change that would ripple through existence for eons to come. The fight was far from over, but for the first time, Shain felt a glimmer of hope, a sense that perhaps, just perhaps, they might win. The Eradicators were gone, but the struggle for freedom, for the right to exist, to remember, to connect, would continue.

The journey had demanded everything, it had been perilous, the choices were agonizing. But they had chosen life, chosen freedom, chosen the messy, unpredictable, beautiful chaos of existence over the sterile, emotionless order imposed by the

Eradicators. And in making that choice, they had changed the universe forever. The universe, though wounded, had not surrendered. It had found its voice again, and it sang not just with pain, but with power. The silence left behind wasn't one of loss. It was the silence before a new symphony.

The song of existence, once nearly silenced, now resonated with a renewed strength, a testament to the enduring power of hope, connection, and the will to resist. And as Shain and Echo looked out at the vast expanse of space, they knew that their journey, their fight, had just begun. The gamble they had taken had changed everything, and the future, though uncertain, held the promise of a universe reborn, free to sing its own song. The silence that remained was not one of defeat, but a prelude to a new song, a song of freedom, resilience, and the enduring power of memory.

Aftermath

The obsidian platform, once the vibrant core of the Eradicators' dominance – now lay still, radiating a faint warmth that felt strangely comforting. The humming, the omnipresent thrum that had permeated their existence for days, had softened, evolving into a low, resonant hum that seemed to vibrate not just through the air, but through the very fabric of reality itself. It was a sound of healing, of regeneration, a cosmic sigh of relief.

Shain raked his fingers through his disheveled hair as the fatigue hit him all at once, not just emotional by physical, like a tidal force crashing into his core. He felt a profound emptiness, a hollow ache that resonated with the silence left in the wake of the confrontation. The weight of his actions, the crushing responsibility of his choices, pressed down on him, threatening to suffocate him.

He had gambled, played a high-stakes game with the fate of the galaxy, and he had won, yet the victory felt hollow, laced with a pervasive sense of unease.

Echo sat quietly beside him, her gaze fixed on the shimmering remnants of the nexus. Her face was etched with a profound

sadness, a weariness that mirrored his own. Her usually vibrant eyes held a haunted quality, as if she were grappling with the enormity of what they had done. The silence between them stretched, heavy with unspoken emotions, the weight of shared experience and the
uncertainty of the future pressing down on them like a physical burden.

"Do you think... we did the right thing?" she finally whispered, her voice barely audible above the low hum.

Shain hesitated, unsure how to answer. The destruction of the nexus had freed the trapped memories of the Iridians, had given voice to the silenced, but at what cost? The Eradicators were gone, their control shattered, but the repercussions of their actions were only beginning to unfurl.

He looked outward, through the vast viewport where stars blinked like ancient eyes, yet the cosmos seemed different, subtly altered, as if the very fabric of reality had been rearranged. The sense of unease, the nagging doubt, intensified. Had they truly liberated the universe, or had they simply unleashed a new, unforeseen chaos?

The days that followed blurred together in whirlwind of effort and motion. The crippled space station slowly began to function, the damaged systems repaired by a tireless team of technicians. The whispers of the Iridians, though fading, continued to resonate within the station's core, a faint echo of their suffering, their resilience, their enduring spirit. Their presence, though intangible, was palpable, a constant reminder of the

consequences of the Eradicators' actions, a testament to their horrific crimes.

Together, Shain and Echo worked tirelessly, poring over the Eradicators' salvaged data, attempting to piece together the organization's motives, their goals, their ultimate purpose. The information they uncovered was fragmented, cryptic, hinting at a level of complexity that defied comprehension. They found evidence of the Eradicators'manipulation of galactic history, their control of information, and their systematic eradication of cultures that refused to submit. They unearthed conspiracies that spanned millennia, networks of influence that extended to the highest levels of galactic power.

The more they learned, the more Shain felt the weight of responsibility on his shoulders. He had saved Echo, had saved the lingering memories of the Iridians, but what about the countless others who had been erased, whose histories had been rewritten, whose existence had been utterly obliterated by the Eradicators?

Layer by layer, Shain uncovered a chilling philosophy: the Eradicators weren't merely deleting civilizations; they were selectively removing specific strands of consciousness, specific patterns of thought, those who posed a threat to their rigid, controlled vision of the universe. Those who embraced empathy, connection, and the free flow of information were systematically targeted. It was a chilling insight into the motives of a civilization that sought to control not only history, but the very nature of reality itself.

The galaxy, once held together by a fragile illusion of order, now teetered on the edge. The whispers of unrest, the rumors of rebellion, grew louder. Old alliances crumbled; new factions emerged, their allegiances shifting like sand dunes in a cosmic wind. The balance of power, carefully maintained by the Eradicators for centuries, was shattered, and the ensuing chaos was breathtaking in its scope and unpredictability.

And in the midst of that storm, Shain and Echo became unwilling icons – a reluctant symbols of rebellion, their actions a catalyst for change, a beacon of hope for those who had been silenced, for those who longed for a universe free from control.

Their story spread like wildfire across the galaxy, inspiring resistance movements, sparking revolutions, igniting a long-dormant flame of defiance. The Eradicators may be gone, but the fight for freedom had just begun. Their victory was merely a turning point, a moment of rupture that had irrevocably altered the course of galactic history.

The consequences of their decision echoed across the stars, reverberating through the tapestry of time itself. They had released the echoes of the erased, shattering the Eradicators' carefully constructed reality, yet the future remained uncertain, a swirling nebula of possibilities, both beautiful and terrifying. The galaxy was theirs to shape, but they were only at the beginning of their work.

The journey wasn't over; it had only just begun. The fight for freedom was far from won. The scars of the Eradicators' reign remained, deep wounds etched into the soul of the galaxy. But

amidst the chaos, the rebuilding, a new song was emerging, a symphony of defiance, resilience, and hope. The universe, wounded but not broken, was singing its own song again, a song of liberty, connection, and the enduring power of memory. But Shain and Echo had made sure it would never be forgotten again. The legacy they left behind was not a simple victory, but a complex tapestry woven from sacrifice, courage, and the indomitable human spirit. The universe was changing, and they were right in the heart of it.

Echos Fate

The hum, once a sinister presence that filled every corridor with dread – had softened into a gentle hum, a lullaby of sorts for a galaxy awakening from a long nightmare. The obsidian platform, once a nexus of control, was inert, its chilling power dissipated. Yet, the silence was not peaceful; it was pregnant with the weight of untold stories, the echoes of silenced voices finally finding their way back into the fabric of reality. Shain felt the reverberations in his bones, a deep, resonating tremor that spoke of loss and liberation in equal measure.

Echo stood at the viewport, her silhouette a stark figure against the glimmering canvas of stars beyond. She was different. The rigid composure she'd maintained throughout their ordeal, the mask of stoic resilience, had cracked, revealing a raw vulnerability that tugged at Shain's heart. Her eyes, usually sparkling with an almost unnerving intensity, were now clouded with a profound sadness, a weariness that seemed to encompass the weight of centuries. The loss of her people, the erasure of their civilization, was a burden she carried with a quiet dignity that both impressed and pained him.

He approached her cautiously, the silence between them thick with unspoken words, shared memories, and the daunting uncertainty of the future. The fight was over, the immediate threat neutralized, but the war, the cosmic struggle for truth and freedom, had only just begun. The galaxy had been irrevocably altered, its equilibrium shattered, and the ripples of change were only just beginning to be felt.

"They're gone," Echo said, her voice a mere whisper, barely audible above the fading hum. "The Eradicators... they're gone." Her statement wasn't a triumph; it was a quiet observation, a recognition of a stark reality, devoid of emotional flourish. The absence of elebratory relief highlighted the enormity of their loss, the gravity of what had been done.

Shain placed a hand on her shoulder and offered her a silent gesture of comfort, of shared understanding. He knew the victory felt hollow, a pyrrhic win bought at a devastating cost. The galaxy was free, yes, but scarred, fractured, wounded. The whispers of the Iridians, though fading, still resonated, a haunting reminder of the atrocities committed, a testament to the resilience of the human spirit in the face of unimaginable horror.

The days that followed were a whirlwind of activity. The crippled space station, a testament to the intensity of their battle, slowly came back to life. Technicians, working tirelessly, repaired damaged systems, their movements fueled by a grim determination to restore some semblance of normalcy to a universe teetering on the brink of chaos. But the whispers persisted, weaving themselves into the very fabric of the station,

a constant reminder of the past, a spectral chorus haunting the present.

Shain and Echo, despite their exhaustion, delved into the Eradicators' salvaged data, a treasure trove of information both horrifying and fascinating. They unearthed details of the organization's meticulous planning, their calculated manipulation of galactic events, their systematic erasure of cultures that dared to challenge their control. They found evidence of influence peddling, of political corruption on a cosmic scale, of conspiracies stretching back millennia. The Eradicators hadn't merely suppressed knowledge; they had rewritten reality itself, shaping the very fabric of galactic history to fit their sinister narrative.

The more they learned, the more terrifying the full scope of the Eradicators' ambitions became. It wasn't merely about power or control; it was about a warped vision of order, a desire to impose a sterile uniformity on a universe teeming with vibrant diversity. They had targeted civilizations not based on their strength or threat level, but on their very nature – their empathy, their capacity for connection, their creative spirit. Those who embraced compassion and understanding were the first to be erased.

The implications were staggering. The galaxy, once seemingly stable under the Eradicators' iron fist, was now a volatile mix of conflicting ideologies, shifting alliances, and simmering rebellions. The fragile peace that had been imposed were shattered now, and the ensuing turmoil threatened to engulf the entire galaxy. The Eradicators were gone, but their legacy of

control and manipulation remained, a festering wound that threatened to poison the future.

Shain and Echo, unknowingly, had become symbols of hope in this chaotic new world. Their actions, their defiance, their struggle for truth had sparked a wave of rebellion, a resurgence of resistance movements across the galaxy. Their story spread like wildfire, fueling the flames of defiance, inspiring others to challenge the oppressive forces that had held them captive for so long. The fight for freedom, they realized, was far from over. It was only just beginning.

Echo's fate remained uncertain. The galactic community, still reeling from the revelation of the Eradicators' crimes and the ensuing chaos, was wary of her, a survivor of a vanished civilization, a symbol of both hope and fear. Some saw her as a beacon of a lost era, a reminder of a time before the Eradicators'reign of terror; others viewed her with suspicion, fearing her unique connection to the cosmic vibrations, the very power that had been weaponized by the Eradicators.

Her future was a blank slate, a canvas onto which the galaxy would paint its own narrative. Would she become a leader, a guide for a new era of galactic unity? Would she choose isolation, seeking solace in the echoes of her lost people? Or would she find a new path, forging her own identity in a universe forever changed by her actions and the actions of those she had fought alongside? The answer lay not in their past victories, but in the choices, they made in uncertain times.

The galaxy had been liberated, but it was also wounded, broken. The responsibility of rebuilding, of healing, of guiding the galaxy towards a future free from the shadow of the Eradicators, now rested squarely on the shoulders of Shain and Echo. They stood on the precipice of a new era, a time of both immense opportunity and profound peril. The legacy of their actions, of the choices they made, would determine the shape of the galaxy for generations to come. The whispers of the erased would guide them, urging them forward into a future where such atrocities would never be repeated, where truth would prevail over manipulation, where the song of freedom would ring out across the cosmos, clear and strong. Their journey had just begun. The galaxy awaited.

Shains Reflection

The rhythmic hum of the restored life support systems resonated through the station, it was a stark contrast to the oppressive silence that had preceded it. The station, once a battleground, now pulsed with a tentative energy, a fragile heartbeat in a galaxy still recovering from its wounds. Yet, despite the quiet rebirth, the echoes of the conflict remained, not just in the physical scars of the station but in the quiet spaces between words, in the lingering tension in the air, in the haunted look in Echo's eyes. Shain found himself staring out at the swirling nebulae, the cosmic canvas painted with hues of vibrant chaos and fragile beauty. It mirrored the turbulent landscape of his own mind.

He had faced down the Eradicators, uncovered and dismantled a conspiracy that had had reshaped the very fabric of the galactic history, and emerged victorious. Or had he? The victory felt hollow, a bitter pill swallowed in the wake of unimaginable loss. The Iridians were gone, erased from existence, their vibrant culture reduced to whispers carried on the cosmic wind. He'd saved Echo, the last ember of their civilization, but the price had been steep. The galaxy was free at a huge cost, it was fractured, wounded, uncertain of its future.

The official reports would spin tales of courage, of decisive action and mission success. Yet Shain knew the reality buried under the wreckage of those summaries. He knew the weight of the silenced voices, the vastness of the loss, the chilling implications of the Eradicators' actions. They hadn't simply suppressed knowledge; they'd attempted to erase entire civilizations, to rewrite the very fabric of reality itself. Their warped vision of order, their desire for a sterile uniformity, had threatened to snuff out the vibrant diversity of the cosmos.

Though the Eradicators had been defeated, the remnants of their ideology still hung like a toxin in the galactic atmosphere. The galactic community was a tinderbox, rife with suspicion and distrust, grappling with the fallout from their deception. Alliances shifted, old loyalties crumbled, and the seeds of new conflicts were sown in the fertile ground of fear and uncertainty. The whispers of the Iridians, faint but persistent, served as a constant reminder of the fragility of existence, the ease with which a civilization could be obliterated, a culture extinguished.

Shain thought of Echo, her quiet strength, her profound sadness. She was a symbol, a living testament to the Eradicators' cruelty, a beacon of hope in a galaxy desperately searching for its footing. He'd seen her vulnerability, the cracks in her stoic façade, the weight of her loss bearing down on her fragile shoulders. Yet, she possessed an inner resilience, a quiet determination that mirrored his own. He found himself drawn to her, not just because of her unique abilities, but because of her shared pain and emotional turmoil.

He had changed, too. The journey had stripped away layers of his own carefully constructed persona, revealing a core of resilience and empathy he didn't know he had. His understanding of life, of existence, had fundamentally shifted. He'd glimpsed the interconnectedness of all things, a cosmic symphony of which the Iridians' song was but a single note. The erasure of that note hadn't silenced the music; it had created a jarring dissonance, a painful reminder of the interconnectedness of all things.

He looked at his hands, calloused and scarred from years of service as a prison marshal. He'd dealt with criminals, with those who had transgressed the laws of society, but the Eradicators were different.

They were not just criminals; they were architects of cosmic control, manipulators of reality. He'd been a cog in the galactic machine, a tool enforcing the laws of a system he now knew to be fundamentally corrupt.

The question gnawed at him: what was the true nature of justice?

Flood of thoughts consume him. Was it merely the enforcement of laws, the upholding of a rigid order, or was it something more profound, something that encompassed compassion, understanding, the preservation of diverse cultures? He realized his previous understanding of justice was simplistic, a naïve approach to a universe vastly more complex than he had ever imagined.

The galaxy's future was uncertain, a tapestry woven with threads of hope and despair, of unity and conflict. The Eradicators were

gone, but their legacy remained, a persistent undercurrent of fear and suspicion. Shain wondered if the galaxy would ever truly heal from its wounds. The whispers of the erased Iridians served as a cautionary tale, a reminder of the fragility of civilizations and the importance of protecting diversity and truth. His role, his duty, was not simply to enforce the laws of a fractured galaxy, but to help guide it towards a future where such atrocities would never be repeated.

The fight, he realized, was far from over. The immediate threat had been neutralized, but the long war for truth and freedom had just begun. The responsibility of rebuilding, of healing, of fostering unity in a fractured galaxy now rested upon his shoulders and Echo's. They were symbols of hope, unwitting leaders of a burgeoning resistance, individuals tasked with navigating a galaxy that had been irrevocably altered. Their story would become a legend, a cautionary tale, and a source of inspiration for generations to come.

Shain didn't pretend to know what lay ahead. He knew the road ahead was long and arduous, fraught with danger and uncertainty. He couldn't predict the future, but he could choose how he responded to it. He would carry forward the lessons of loss and the wisdom, hard-earned knowledge, to guide the galaxy towards a brighter future, a future where the song of freedom could ring out, clear and strong, across the cosmos. He would honor the memory of the lost, and he would fight to ensure that their sacrifices would not be in vain. The galaxy awaited, and he would meet its challenges with a renewed sense of purpose, but also lit with the enduring flame of hope. This was not the end of the story, but the beginning of another – a story of healing, of

rebuilding, of leading the galaxy towards a future free from the shadow of the Eradicators. The whispers of the erased would guide him, and their song would become the soundtrack of his future.

Whispers of the Future

The void thrummed—a low, resonant hum that reverberated not just in the ship's hull but deep within Shain's bones. Beyond the viewport, the nebula, once a chaotic swirl of vibrant colors, now seemed subdued, muted, as if the cosmos had collectively sighed in exhaustion. The victory over the Eradicators felt less like triumph and more like a reprieve, a temporary pause in a cosmic war whose boundaries remained undefined. He looked at Echo, who sat bathed in the ethereal glow of the nebula, her eyes closed, a faint smile playing on her lips. She seemed to be listening to something, something beyond the reach of his senses.

"What is it?" Shain asked, his voice a hushed thread.

Echo opened her eyes, their depths mirroring the vastness of space. "The song," she said, her voice soft, almost inaudible. "It's… different."

"Different how?"

"It's… incomplete now. Where there was once unbroken melody, there are silences. But… new notes are emerging. Faint, tentative, but there." She gestured towards the nebula, as if the cosmic tapestry itself were playing a symphony only she could hear.

"The universe is healing, Shain. But it's a slow process, a long recovery. The scars remain, but new life is growing around them."

Shain absorbed her words. The Eradicators had tried to erase the Iridians, to smother their song, to rewrite reality itself. But reality, it seemed, was far more resilient than they had imagined. The universe didn't simply accept erasure; it adapted, it found new ways to express itself, to continue its existence. The whispers of the erased Iridians, once a mournful lament, now held a subtle note of defiance, a testament to the enduring power of life.

Days blurred into weeks, weeks into months. Their journey across the galaxy unfolded—not as fugitives, but as reluctant ambassadors of a new era. Echo's unique ability to perceive the cosmic vibrations, to listen to the universe's symphony, proved invaluable. She could sense disturbances in the cosmic fabric, anomalies that hinted at hidden dangers, forgotten secrets. She led them to forgotten worlds, to lost civilizations, to places where the whispers of the past were still audible.

One such world was Xylos, cloaked in perpetual dusk, where the air itself vibrated with dormant energy. There, they uncovered an ancient archive, meticulously maintained by a reclusive order of keepers—descendants of those who had resisted the Eradicators, guarding their knowledge jealously. They distrusted outsiders, viewing them with suspicion. Shain had to navigate a delicate dance of trust, earning their confidence slowly, proving his commitment to preserving, not exploiting, the knowledge they possessed. The experience challenged his preconceived

notions of security and control, forcing him to rely on diplomacy and empathy rather than force.

Within the archive's depths, they unearthed fragments of Iridian history: lost songs, forgotten rituals, insights into their intricate cosmology. The archive was a treasure trove, a testament to the resilience of Iridian ingenuity. Shain's hands trembled as he handled a crystalline tablet, its surface etched with symbols that pulsed in time with the Iridian song. Echo's eyes widened, recognizing the Resonance Codex—a ritual that wove the song into relics like the Resonance Key, Echo Stone, Pulse Shard, and Star Veil.

Their journey wasn't confined to physical locations. Echo's perception of cosmic vibrations gave them a new window into the universe's workings. They began to understand the deep interconnectedness of all things, the subtle ways in which every event rippled outwards, influencing others across vast distances and time. This understanding challenged Shain's linear view of time and causality, transforming his perception of reality itself.

They encountered other survivors of the Eradicators' purges, scattered remnants of civilizations thought lost. Each meeting revealed new aspects of the Eradicators' ambitions: they hadn't merely sought to suppress knowledge but to impose a sterile, uniform order on the universe, eliminating all diversity and dissent.

The cosmic vibrations were shifting. The song of the universe, once disrupted by the Eradicators' actions, was slowly reassembling itself. New notes were emerging, melodies that

spoke of resilience, of adaptation, of the enduring power of life. The whispers of the erased were no longer mere echoes of loss; they were becoming voices of hope, guiding the galaxy toward a new dawn.

Amid their discoveries, a darker truth surfaced: the Eradicators weren't entirely gone. Their technology, their ideology, remained embedded in the galactic infrastructure, subtly influencing events, shaping the course of history from the shadows. It was a fight not just against a visible enemy but against an insidious network of control that extended into the very fabric of reality. This realization fueled a renewed sense of urgency in Shain and Echo. Their journey had become a crusade to cleanse the galaxy of the Eradicators' legacy, to build a future free from their oppressive influence.

Shain found himself increasingly drawn to Echo's worldview, her profound understanding of the universe's interdependence. He began to question the foundations of his own beliefs, challenging the rigid structure of galactic law and order he had once blindly upheld. His perspective shifted from one of a law enforcer to that of a protector, a guardian of diversity and truth. The galaxy's future, he realized, wasn't just about enforcing rules but about fostering harmony and understanding among different cultures.

Their journey was one of transformation. Shain, once a hardened prison marshal, found himself emerging as a leader, a champion of freedom, a beacon of hope in a galaxy struggling to heal its wounds. Echo, burdened by the loss of her people, discovered her own resilience, her own strength, her own purpose. Together, they were crafting a new reality, a future where the voices of the

erased would be heard, their songs celebrated, their memory honored.

The whispers of the future were no longer mere murmurs in the dark; they were becoming a symphony, a testament to the enduring power of life in the face of oblivion. The universe hummed, its song ever-evolving, and they, Shain and Echo, would be a part of it. The struggle continued, but the whispers of the future held the promise of a song worth fighting for.

Shain stood on the Starseeker's bridge, the hum of the ship's damaged systems blending with the Iridian song. The revelations from prior chapters—Kaelis's betrayal, Veyra's shadow, Silentium's reach, the Pulse Shard, the Star Veil, the Resonance Binding, the Cosmic Weaving, the Eradicators' archive, the voices of the fallen, Echo's role as the last spark, Shain's resolve, the reality-manipulation engine, their alliance, and the nebula chase—wove a tapestry of dread and purpose. His mind drifted to Elyra, a planet of harmonic tides where he'd arrested a mystic, Taryn Thal, who'd spoken of the Resonance Codex. Elyra's tides were erased in a "gravitational surge," Taryn's teachings buried. Now, her words echoed in the archive's crystals, urging him to act.

He approached the Xylos keepers, their leader, an elder named Zara, eyeing him warily. "Why should we trust you, outsider?" she demanded, her voice sharp as the crystal spires around them. Shain knelt, offering the reality-manipulation device. "We're fighting the Eradicators, who silenced your ancestors. This device is their weapon. Help us use the Codex to stop them."

Zara's eyes softened, sensing the song's pulse in the device. "The Codex binds us to the cosmic web," she said. "It's in the Key, hidden in Valthara's rift. But Silentium's agents watch us."

Shain's pulse quickened. The Resonance Key could restore the song. He called Jax and Rix to the archive, their faces weary but determined. "The Codex," Shain said, sharing Zara's words. "It's our weapon against the Eradicators. We need the Key, but Silentium's here."

Jax's eyes widened, his hand tightening on his rifle. "Sir, I felt it— the song. In the archive, it was like it was singing through me. It's real, but it's heavy, pulling me somewhere."

Rix nodded, his voice tense. "The ship's sensors are picking up a signal, sir. It's syncing with the nebula, disrupting ORION's core. I found another subroutine—Silentium's code, rerouting our comms to an Eradicator beacon."

Shain's stomach twisted. He accessed the Starseeker's archives, digging for references to the Resonance Codex. A redacted file surfaced, labeled "Veil Protocol: Eternal Void," detailing a Council operation to suppress harmonic relics. Elyra, Sylara, Voryn—all targeted, all erased. The Resonance Key was listed as a "cosmic disruptor," capable of amplifying the song to shatter Silentium's control. Veyra was its hunter, her rogue status a cover for her Eradicator allegiance.

Shain shared the file with Echo and Zara. "The Key—it's in Valthara's rift, with the Silent Choir. But Veyra's vessel is tracking us. How do we use the Codex?"

Echo's voice was a soft hum, resonating with the archive's crystals. "The Codex is our shield, Shain. It weaves us to the song, to each other. The Choir will guide us, but Silentium's agents are among you. Trust the song, but watch your crew."

Her words chilled him. Kaelis, Vorn, Lira, Vara, Taryn, Myra— how many more were compromised? He ordered Rix to scan the ship for Silentium's code, fearing another infiltrator. The scan revealed a micro-device in the navigation array, pulsing with Eradicator runes, steering them toward an ambush. "Another saboteur," Shain muttered, sprinting to the nav bay with Jax.

There, Ensign Myra stood by the controls, her eyes glassy, a device in her hand. "Myra, stop!" Shain shouted, his pistol raised. Her voice was mechanical: "The Silence demands her." Jax tackled her, Shain disabling the device, but the nav system flickered, threatening to strand them. Alarms blared, the nebula's pulse surging outside, the air crackling with energy.

Echo's voice came through the comms, calm but urgent. "Sing, Shain. The Key's rhythm can stabilize it." Jax and Shain hummed, their voices unsteady but growing stronger, syncing with the rift's pulse. Echo and Zara joined, their harmony weaving through the ship, stabilizing the system. Myra collapsed, her eyes clearing. "Veyra... she's in the rift," she gasped.

Shain restrained Myra, his mind reeling. Silentium's implants were pervasive, Veyra's influence a shadow in their minds. He returned to the bridge, where an alarm blared: "Vessel detected—Silentium signature." The sensors showed the

obsidian Eradicator ship, its hull etched with runes, broadcasting Veyra's voice: "Surrender the Iridian, or the Key is ours."

Shain's hand hovered over the weapons console, but Echo's voice stopped him. "The song, Shain. It's our shield." Jax, Rix, Echo, and Zara sang, their harmony resonating through the ship, disrupting the vessel's systems. Shain joined, the vibration shaking his core, forcing the ship to retreat into the nebula's mists.

The crew's tension flared, whispers of mutiny resurfacing. Ensign Vara's voice echoed: "She's controlling us!" Shain silenced her, his voice firm. "The song's saving us, Vara. The Eradicators are the threat." He ordered neural scans, revealing no new implants, but the crew's fear of the song grew, a fracture he couldn't mend.

A new transmission arrived, untraceable, from the Silent Choir: "Starseeker, the Key sings in Valthara's rift. Encode it with the Codex, or Silentium consumes all." Shain shared it with Jax, Rix, and Zara, their resolve strengthening. "We're in, sir," Jax said, his voice steady. "For the song."

The Starseeker limped through the hidden system, its systems barely functional. ORION's voice crackled: "Anomaly detected— rift core unstable." Shain pulled up the sensors, spotting a shimmering vortex in the nebula, its rhythm chaotic, corrupted by Silentium. Echo's voice guided them: "Sing through it, Shain. The Key's there."

Shain, Jax, Rix, and Zara sang, their voices weaving with Echo's, stabilizing the vortex. The Resonance Key's pulse emerged, a

beacon to Valthara. Shain's heart pounded—he was no longer just a marshal, but a singer, carrying the Iridian song against a galaxy that sought to silence it.

The journey through the Sylaran Nebula remained perilous, the rift's sentient pulse amplifying the song's effects. Shain's memories surged—Taryn Thal's teachings, Lirien Vex's verses, Myra Vex's research—all pointing to the song's power. He sat with Echo and Zara, their calm anchoring him. "Tell me about the Resonance Codex," he said. "How does it restore the song?"

Echo's voice was a melody, weaving through the hum. "The Codex is a vow, Shain. Iridians encoded their essence into the relics, tying them to the cosmic web. The Key amplifies, the Stone remembers, the Shard guides, the Veil protects. Together, they can restore the song, awaken the galaxy. Valthara's choir awaits, but Veyra's vessel is closing in."

Zara nodded, her voice steady. "The archive holds the Codex's fragments. Use them to encode the Key, but beware—Silentium's network lingers in the rift."

Shain's resolve hardened. He recalled Elyra's tides, their harmonic glow fading under Council fire. "Can we encode it? Here, now?"

Echo's smile was faint but resolute. "You're already encoding, Shain. You, Jax, Rix, Zara—you're part of the song. Trust it, and it'll guide us to Valthara."

The crew's unrest lingered, fear of the song spreading. Shain faced a dilemma: amplify the song through the ship's systems,

risking Silentium's detection, or trust the Choir's guidance to Valthara. He shared the choice with Echo and Zara. "Amplifying it could counter Veyra's vessel," he said. "But it might expose us."

Echo's eyes gleamed. "The song is our truth, Shain. Amplify it, but trust the Choir. They'll protect us."

Shain rerouted power to the comms array, amplifying the song's pulse. The Starseeker vibrated, the nebula's rift glowing brighter, but Veyra's vessel returned, its runes pulsing. Shain, Jax, Rix, Echo, and Zara sang, their harmony a shield, forcing the vessel to retreat. The Key's pulse grew, guiding them to Valthara, the song's truth their only hope.

Shain's memories of Elyra resurfaced—nights studying Taryn's teachings, her warnings about the Eradicators' reach. The song echoed those warnings, a truth he'd buried under years of duty. On the bridge, the nebula's mists swirled, and Shain felt the song's presence—not just in Echo, but in himself, in Jax, in Rix, in Zara, in the Starseeker's hum. The Eradicators sought to silence it, but Shain, the reluctant marshal, was now its conductor, determined to let the galaxy hear its melody.

Enduring Legacy

The rhythmic thrum of the hyperdrive gradually faded, leaving behind the quiet hum of the ship's life support systems. Where silence had once been a source of dread, it now felt... comforting. A stark contrast to the cacophony of the battle against the Eradicators, the aftermath left a strange peace in its wake. Shain stared out at the swirling nebula, its colors now vibrant and full, not muted as they had been during their flight. It felt as though the very fabric of space had breathed a sigh of relief.

Echo sat beside him in quiet contemplation, her fingertips absentmindedly tracing patterns on the armrest, her eyes closed. The cosmic vibrations, the symphony she perceived, were different now. The mournful undertones, the echoes of loss from the silenced Iridians, were still present, but they were interwoven with a new melody, a hopeful counterpoint. It was a fragile sound, almost imperceptible, yet undeniably there. A song of rebirth.

"It's growing stronger," she murmured, her voice barely louder than the ship's gentle hum. "The song... it's weaving itself back together."

Shain nodded, a quiet understanding passing between them. The Eradicators had tried to erase the Iridians, to sever the connection, to silence the song. They had failed. The universe, it seemed, was far too resilient, too interconnected, to be so easily subjugated. The act of silencing a civilization did not silence its legacy. Their essence, their spirit, their song, lived on, manifested in the subtle shifts of cosmic vibrations, in the faint whispers across the galaxy.

Their journey continued, but now it felt not like a desperate flight from pursuers, but a pilgrimage, a quest to understand the deeper implications of what they had uncovered. Each new system they visited held echoes of the Iridian song, subtle harmonies and dissonances that spoke of their influence, their legacy. They found small pockets of resistance, hidden communities who had survived the Eradicators' purge, clinging to their cultural heritage, whispering tales of survival and resistance passed down through generations.

On the luminous world of Aethel, perpetually basking in the warm embrace of twin suns, they encountered the descendants of a species the Eradicators had nearly wiped out. Their culture had been reduced to fragments, scattered memories passed down through generations, a few surviving artifacts bearing testament to their once-vibrant civilization. Yet, within those fragments, they discovered an astonishing resilience, a tenacity to preserve their identity, a determination to rebuild from the ashes of destruction. Their story, interwoven with the Iridian song, spoke of endurance, adaptation, and the enduring strength of the spirit, irrespective of form.

Echo's unique ability to perceive the cosmic vibrations proved invaluable. She could sense the lingering effects of the Eradicators' technology, the subtle distortions in the fabric of reality they had created. She guided them to hidden caches of knowledge, to forgotten archives, to places where the whispers of the past still resonated, revealing more about the Eradicators' plans, their ultimate goals, and the devastating impact of their attempts at control.

They discovered the Eradicators hadn't just sought to erase civilizations; their true goal was to homogenize the galaxy, to impose a singular, uniform culture, eliminating all diversity, all individuality. They saw the universe not as a vibrant symphony of diverse voices, but as a monotonous drone to be controlled.

Their journey led them to the heart of the Eradicators' command—an abandoned world ravaged by centuries of conflict. Here, amidst the ruins, they found not only the remnants of the Eradicators' technology but also a chilling record of their actions. A comprehensive database, meticulously documenting their methods, their targets, their reasons. The sheer scale of their cruelty was staggering, a stark reminder of the danger of unchecked power and the insidious nature of totalitarian ideologies.

The database also revealed a chilling truth—one that challenged their assumptions about the Eradicators. Their actions, though ruthless, had not been born solely from malice, but from a deep-seated fear. A fear of chaos, of diversity, of the unpredictable nature of existence. They believed their control was necessary to maintain order, to prevent the collapse of the galaxy into

anarchy. Their misguided attempts at control only created a far greater chaos, tearing apart the fabric of reality itself.

The discovery delivered a sobering insight into the fragility of civilizations, the ease with which even the most powerful can be consumed by their own fears and insecurities. It served as a stark warning against the dangers of suppressing individuality and diversity. It also provided some understanding, though not justification, for their actions.

However, their journey wasn't solely about confronting the past. It was about creating a future, a future where the song of the universe could be sung freely, where diversity was celebrated, and where the lessons of the past served as a guide, not a prison. They worked tirelessly to dismantle the remaining vestiges of the Eradicators' influence, exposing their hidden machinations, and empowering those who had been silenced. They shared the Iridian song, its fragments of hope, with all who would listen.

The journey's end didn't come with triumph or fanfare. There were no banners raised, no decisive victory declared. Instead, there came a quiet understanding, a calm acknowledgment of what had been accomplished and what remained undone. The Eradicators' influence might have been diminished, but their ideology, the seeds of their control, would likely linger in the shadows of the galaxy. The fight was not over, but the hope was palpable. The whispers had grown into a chorus, a symphony of defiance against the attempts to erase the memories, the identities, and the songs of diverse peoples. The melody, though still fragile, was strong.

The Iridian song, once a lament for a lost civilization, had become a hymn for resilience. It was a testament to the enduring power of life, a melody weaving together the threads of hope, memory, and a shared future—a symphony of survival and remembrance. Their journey showed the universe's incredible ability to adapt, to heal, to create new harmonies from the shards of the past. Shain and Echo, together, had become the conductors of this new symphony, ensuring that the voices of the erased would never be truly silent, their legacy eternally woven into the fabric of the cosmos. The universe itself seemed to sing in response—ever-changing, ever-growing. A song that embraced complexity, honored the past, and looked forward with cautious but undaunted hope. It was a living affirmation of the strength found in difference, in collaboration, in spirit. Though the road ahead remained unwritten and its end unknown, one thing was certain: the music continued.

Shain stood on the Starseeker's bridge, the hum of the ship's systems blending with the Iridian song. The revelations from prior chapters—Kaelis's betrayal, Veyra's shadow, Silentium's reach, the Pulse Shard, the Star Veil, the Resonance Binding, the Cosmic Weaving, the Eradicators' archive, the voices of the fallen, Echo's role as the last spark, Shain's resolve, the reality-manipulation engine, their alliance, the nebula chase, and the Xylos archive—wove a tapestry of dread and purpose. His mind drifted to Thalara, a planet of harmonic winds where he'd arrested a sage, Elara Vyn, who'd spoken of the Resonance Codex. Thalara's winds were erased in a "quantum storm," Elara's teachings buried. Now, her wisdom echoed in Aethel's artifacts, urging him to act.

He approached the Aethel survivors, their leader, a mystic named Kalia, eyeing him warily. "Why should we trust you, outsider?" she demanded, her voice sharp as the twin suns' light. Shain knelt, offering a crystalline artifact from Xylos. "We're fighting the Eradicators, who silenced your ancestors. This holds the Codex. Help us use it to stop them."

Kalia's eyes softened, sensing the song's pulse in the artifact. "The Codex binds us to the cosmic web," she said. "It's in the Key, hidden in Valthara's rift. But Silentium's agents watch us."

Shain's pulse quickened. The Resonance Key could restore the song. He called Jax and Rix to the archive, their faces weary but determined. "The Codex," Shain said, sharing Kalia's words. "It's our weapon against the Eradicators. We need the Key, but Silentium's here."

Jax's eyes widened, his hand tightening on his rifle. "Sir, I felt it—the song. In Aethel's ruins, it was like it was singing through me. It's real, but it's heavy, pulling me somewhere."

Rix nodded, his voice tense. "The ship's sensors are picking up a signal, sir. It's syncing with the nebula, disrupting ORION's core. I found another subroutine—Silentium's code, rerouting our power systems to an Eradicator beacon."

Shain's stomach twisted. He accessed the Starseeker's archives, digging for references to the Resonance Codex. A redacted file surfaced, labeled "Veil Protocol: Silent Eternity," detailing a Council operation to suppress harmonic relics. Thalara, Elyra, Sylara—all targeted, all erased. The Resonance Key was listed as

a "cosmic disruptor," capable of amplifying the song to shatter Silentium's control. Veyra was its hunter, her rogue status a cover for her Eradicator allegiance.

Shain shared the file with Echo and Kalia. "The Key—it's in Valthara's rift, with the Silent Choir. But Veyra's vessel is tracking us. How do we use the Codex?"

Echo's voice was a soft hum, resonating with the artifact's pulse. "The Codex is our shield, Shain. It weaves us to the song, to each other. The Choir will guide us, but Silentium's agents are among you. Trust the song, but watch your crew."

Her words chilled him. Kaelis, Vorn, Lira, Vara, Taryn, Myra— how many more were compromised? He ordered Rix to scan the ship for Silentium's code, fearing another infiltrator. The scan revealed a micro-device in the propulsion array, pulsing with Eradicator runes, draining their engines. "Another saboteur," Shain muttered, sprinting to the propulsion bay with Jax.

There, Ensign Lira stood by the controls, her eyes glassy, a device in her hand. "Lira, stop!" Shain shouted, his pistol raised. Her voice was mechanical: "The Silence demands her." Jax tackled her, Shain disabling the device, but the engines flickered, threatening to stall. Alarms blared, the nebula's pulse surging outside, the air crackling with energy.

Echo's voice came through the comms, calm but urgent. "Sing, Shain. The Key's rhythm can stabilize it." Jax and Shain hummed, their voices unsteady but growing stronger, syncing with the rift's pulse. Echo and Kalia joined, their harmony weaving

through the ship, stabilizing the system. Lira collapsed, her eyes clearing. "Veyra... she's in the rift," she gasped.

Shain restrained Lira, his mind reeling. Silentium's implants were pervasive, Veyra's influence a shadow in their minds. He returned to the bridge, where an alarm blared: "Vessel detected—Silentium signature." The sensors showed the obsidian Eradicator ship, its hull etched with runes, broadcasting Veyra's voice: "Surrender the Iridian, or the Key is ours."

Shain's hand hovered over the weapons console, but Echo's voice stopped him. "The song, Shain. It's our shield." Jax, Rix, Echo, and Kalia sang, their harmony resonating through the ship, disrupting the vessel's systems. Shain joined, the vibration shaking his core, forcing the ship to retreat into the nebula's mists.

The crew's tension flared, whispers of mutiny resurfacing. Ensign Vara's voice echoed: "She's controlling us!" Shain silenced her, his voice firm. "The song's saving us, Vara. The Eradicators are the threat." He ordered neural scans, revealing no new implants, but the crew's fear of the song grew, a fracture he couldn't mend.

A new transmission arrived, untraceable, from the Silent Choir: "Starseeker, the Key sings in Valthara's rift. Encode it with the Codex, or Silentium consumes all." Shain shared it with Jax, Rix, and Kalia, their resolve strengthening. "We're in, sir," Jax said, his voice steady. "For the song."

The Starseeker limped through the hidden system, its systems barely functional. ORION's voice crackled: "Anomaly detected—rift core unstable." Shain pulled up the sensors, spotting a shimmering vortex in the nebula, its rhythm chaotic, corrupted by Silentium. Echo's voice guided them: "Sing through it, Shain. The Key's there."

Shain, Jax, Rix, and Kalia sang, their voices weaving with Echo's, stabilizing the vortex. The Resonance Key's pulse emerged, a beacon to Valthara. Shain's heart pounded—he was no longer just a marshal, but a singer, carrying the Iridian song against a galaxy that sought to silence it.

The journey through the Sylaran Nebula remained perilous, the rift's sentient pulse amplifying the song's effects. Shain's memories surged—Elara Vyn's teachings, Taryn Thal's wisdom, Lirien Vex's verses—all pointing to the song's power. He sat with Echo and Kalia, their calm anchoring him. "Tell me about the Resonance Codex," he said. "How does it restore the song?"

Echo's voice was a melody, weaving through the hum. "The Codex is a vow, Shain. Iridians encoded their essence into the relics, tying them to the cosmic web. The Key amplifies, the Stone remembers, the Shard guides, the Veil protects. Together, they can restore the song, awaken the galaxy. Valthara's choir awaits, but Veyra's vessel is closing in."

Kalia nodded, her voice steady. "Aethel's artifacts hold the Codex's fragments. Use them to encode the Key, but beware—Silentium's network lingers in the rift."

Shain's resolve hardened. He recalled Thalara's winds, their harmonic glow fading under Council fire. "Can we encode it? Here, now?"

Echo's smile was faint but resolute. "You're already encoding, Shain. You, Jax, Rix, Kalia—you're part of the song. Trust it, and it'll guide us to Valthara."

The crew's unrest lingered, fear of the song spreading. Shain faced a dilemma: amplify the song through the ship's systems, risking Silentium's detection, or trust the Choir's guidance to Valthara. He shared the choice with Echo and Kalia. "Amplifying it could counter Veyra's vessel," he said. "But it might expose us."

Echo's eyes gleamed. "The song is our truth, Shain. Amplify it, but trust the Choir. They'll protect us."

Shain rerouted power to the comms array, amplifying the song's pulse. The Starseeker vibrated, the nebula's rift glowing brighter, but Veyra's vessel returned, its runes pulsing. Shain, Jax, Rix, Echo, and Kalia sang, their harmony a shield, forcing the vessel to retreat. The Key's pulse grew, guiding them to Valthara, the song's truth their only hope.

Shain's memories of Thalara resurfaced—nights studying Elara's teachings, her warnings about the Eradicators' reach. The song echoed those warnings, a truth he'd buried under years of duty. On the bridge, the nebula's mists swirled, and Shain felt the song's presence—not just in Echo, but in himself, in Jax, in Rix, in Kalia, in the Starseeker's hum. The Eradicators sought to silence

it, but Shain, the reluctant marshal, was now its conductor, determined to let the galaxy hear its melody.

Acknowledgments

My deepest gratitude goes to my wife, whose unwavering support and insightful feedback have been my compass through every stage of his work. To my editor Sarah Chen, whose expertise and patience guided me. To Author's Point for the opportunity to share my vision and guide me through the final stages, thank you for believing in this story. Finally, to my friends and family who have supported my work, your enthusiasm is the fuel that drives my creativity.

Appendix

i: Dust and Whispers

A War of Whispers, the unofficial name of it, for the way it spread through the star systems, not with the roar of cannons or the blinding flash of nova bombs, but with anxieties and suspicions that festered into outright hatred. It started, as most wars do, with a resource scarcity, a desperate scramble for the dwindling reserves that

powered the hyperdrives and kept the galactic economy humming.
glittering domes interconnected by shimmering transit tubes, pulsed with quiet energy. There were no towering monuments to war, no grim reminders of past conflicts. Only sculptures that whispered of it ended, not with a victor, but with a graveyard of civilizations, some extinguished completely, others clinging to existence by the thread of a single, solitary life.

Now, the dust was settling, and the Universal Council, a fractured and weary body, was attempting to rebuild. But the wounds ran deep. The desire for retribution, for eradication, burned hotter than any supernova. Every species, every individual,

was judged, weighed, and found wanting. Those deemed worthy of continued existence, were protected, albeit reluctantly. But there were others... Those shadowed by doubt, suspicion, or outright accusation were held in limbo, their fates uncertain. The most dangerous of these were the Singularities, the sole survivors of vanished races. Their continued existence represented a threat, a lingering reminder of the horrors of the war. Fear, more than any logical argument, dictated their confinement.

ii: People of Luna Minor

From orbit, Luna Minor was a sapphire marble veined with silver, a testament to the sophisticated atmospheric processors that kept its thin air breathable. On the surface, the cities of the Iridians,
glittering domes interconnected by shimmering transit tubes, pulsed with quiet energy. There were no towering monuments to war, no grim reminders of past conflicts. Only sculptures that whispered of harmony, gardens that echoed with the music of alien birds, and libraries filled with the accumulated wisdom of generations.

The Iridians, all 200,000 of them, lived lives devoted to the pursuit of knowledge and beauty. Their days were filled with studying holographic simulations of nebulae, debating the finer points of abstract art, or unraveling the complex algorithms that governed the simulated ecosystems within their domes. They prized intellectual curiosity above all else. Birthdays were celebrated not with gifts, but with the presentation of a complex philosophical problem to be pondered for the coming year.

Their science was advanced, bordering on the mystical. They had mastered manipulation of gravitational fields on a small scale, allowing for cities that gently floated just above the surface of the moon. They had unlocked the secrets of near-instantaneous communication, using quantum entanglement to transmit thoughts and ideas across vast distances. But their science was always tempered by an unwavering ethical code. They understood the potential dangers of their discoveries and approached each new breakthrough with cautious reverence.

Their art reflected this delicate balance. Sculptures shifted and flowed with the ambient light, changing shape and color according to the viewer's emotional state. Music was composed using algorithms that predicted emotional resonance, creating harmonies that spoke directly to the soul. Even their architecture was designed to inspire contemplation, with flowing lines and open spaces that encouraged introspection.

Philosophy was the cornerstone of Iridian life. They explored the nature of consciousness, the meaning of existence, and the complex relationship between the individual and the collective. They had developed a sophisticated system of ethics based on empathy and understanding, striving to see the world through the eyes of others. For centuries, the Iridians thrived in their peaceful isolation. They were content to observe the universe from afar, contributing their knowledge and art to the cosmic tapestry without seeking recognition or reward. The universe, however, had other plans. A small blip on a long-range sensor, a flicker in the otherwise silent expanse of space. A signal. A signal that meant they were no longer alone. And the delicate balance of their utopian world was about to be tested. Will a society built

on peace and intellect survive contact with a galaxy far less enlightened? Only time would tell.

Glossary

Eradicators: A shadowy organization dedicated to eliminating diverse cultures and imposing a singular galactic culture.

Iridians: A technologically advanced civilization inhabiting Luna Minor, known for their ability to perceive and manipulate cosmic vibrations.

Cosmic Vibrations: Subtle energy patterns that form the basis of Iridian culture and technology. These vibrations are perceived as a complex "song" by the Iridians.

Hyperdrive: A faster-than-light propulsion system used for interstellar travel.

Containment Zone: A highly secure facility designed to isolate individuals posing a threat to galactic stability.

References

While this novel is a work of fiction, the following sources provided inspiration and background material:

The Science of Interstellar

by Kip Thorne

Quantum Physics for Beginners : The Non-Scientist's Guide to the Big Ideas of Quantum Mechanics, with Key Principles, Major Theories, and Experiments Simplified by Pantheon Space Academy

Alien Earths: The New Science of Planet Hunting in the Cosmos

by Dr. Lisa Kaltenegger

Author Biography

EX Katsaros is a science fiction author specializing in speculative fiction that explores themes of memory, loss, and the nature of reality. He works often blends elements of mystery, thriller, and philosophical inquiry, delving into the complexities of human experience within a vast and often unpredictable realms.

EX Katsaros holds a degree in biochemistry, neurobiology and abnormal psychology. He has spent considerable time researching the cultural impacts of advanced technology and interstellar exploration. This research is reflected in the intricate and thought-provoking narratives. This his fist full novel. Previous works include scientific studies and short stories. EX Katsaros currently resides in southern California, where he continues to craft captivating and scientifically informed stories, hopefully to bring a new aspect to the genre.